I0593914

BETRAYED

BOOK THREE IN THE VAEDRA CHRONICLES
SERIES

ESTER LÓPEZ

Writing & Photographic Services LLC

PUBLISHED BY
Writing & Photographic Services, LLC

Writing & Photographic Services LLC

BETRAYED
Copyright © 2019 by ESTER LÓPEZ

All characters in this book are fictitious and any resemblance to actual persons living or dead, places, events, or locales is purely coincidental.

This book may not be reproduced, scanned, or distributed in any printed or electronic form without permission from the author, except for brief quotations embodied in reviews. Please do not participate in or encourage piracy of copyrighted materials in violation of the author's rights. All characters and storylines are the property of the author and your support and respect is appreciated.

This book contains mature content and is intended for adult readers.
Cover Design by ebooklaunch.com
ISBN: 978-0-9970033-4-5

DEDICATION

For my daughter, Bridget, who is the inspiration for
Keely McGuire.

SOCIAL MEDIA

To keep up to date on the author's book releases and book signings, please join Ester's Readers Group at: www.esterlopez.com

Follow Ester's Blogs at:

www.esterlopez.com
www.AuthorBlogSpot.esterlopez.com

Follow Ester on:

Twitter @esterlopez1
Facebook as EsterLopezAuthor

And if you like the story, please give an honest review at Amazon.com or Goodreads.com

1

PLANET EARTH

WASHINGTON, D.C.

*W*as it wrong to pray that nothing happened every day?

Keely McGuire sat in the back of the briefing room while Gowan went over assignment changes. She prayed her assignment stayed the same. She had been at the White House a year now and still felt like a rookie. Gowan had finished talking and hadn't called her name. While other agents got up to leave, she headed to the front of the room to check her assignment. Gowan spoke to another agent away from the desk. She ran her finger down the page. Good. She was assigned to the Oval Office again today.

A heavy hand rested on her shoulder. She straightened and turned. Gowan.

"Yes, you still have Oval Office duty."

"Thank you, sir," she managed to say.

"I'm surprised, McGuire."

"Oh?"

"Most agents look forward to a change in duty at least every now and then. Sometimes they even ask for a change, but not you. Why is that?"

"I like where I'm at, sir."

"Do you, McGuire?"

She swallowed hard and nodded. She couldn't get away fast enough. When she got to the Oval Office, she straightened her bulletproof vest and checked her holster to make sure her Sig was in place. She didn't care that other agents got promotions or moved on to other assignments. She liked where she was. It was safe.

When her shift ended, she offered another prayer of thanks for an uneventful day. She checked her watch. Her parents had invited her over for the weekend. She hadn't seen them in a month and looked forward to the visit.

Her cell phone rang as she got into her car.

"Hello, David, how was your day?" she asked.

"I got a new lead on a story I've been working on. How about you? Did you wear that new ring I bought you?"

"My day was quiet as usual. I'm sorry, but I forgot to wear the ring. I promise I'll wear it next week."

"Good. Be sure that you do. I just can't believe you work at the White House and nothing ever happens around there."

"I'm sure things happen there, I'm just not at the scene where it does."

"Is this the weekend you're heading into Virginia to see your parents?"

"Yes. Would you like to join me? I'm sure they'd love to meet you."

"Maybe some other time. I'll be hanging out with the boys this weekend. You have fun. I'll see you when you get back."

Keely set her phone in the seat next to her then pulled off her vest. Although she had been seeing David for nearly a month, she didn't feel comfortable sharing what her career entailed. After all, he worked for a local newspaper, writing about life in Washington, DC. She was a Secret

Service agent and secrets were part of her life. Their motto was "Worthy of Trust and Confidence." She wasn't sure how much she could trust David yet. As far as David knew, she was an intern in the Office of Public Liaison through the White House internship program. She actually had worked there briefly while waiting to be accepted by the Secret Service.

It was probably good that he decided not to take her up on her offer. Her mother didn't like him, and she hadn't even met him.

She put the top down on her convertible and pulled her hair loose from the tight bun she wore while she worked. Since she had packed her bags earlier this morning, she headed south to Virginia. This weekend she had to tell them she was having second thoughts on her career choice.

2

VIRGINIA COUNTRYSIDE

*K*eely McGuire stared through the eyepiece of her father's telescope. It sat on the back deck of the house. A cloudless night, and the telescope was pointed at the moon. She enjoyed spending time with her parents in the quiet countryside, away from the hectic pace of Washington, D.C.

"What am I supposed to see, Dad?" His sudden interest in stargazing surprised her since his only hobbies were fishing and hunting.

"Just look at the moon long enough and you may see a flash of light shooting out." He stood a few feet away and coached her.

"Yeah, I just saw one! What is it?" A pang of excitement hit her as the powerful telescope enabled her to see the flash.

"I think they're UFOs."

Keely straightened. "Really?" She shoved her hands into her jean's pockets. A shiver ran down her spine. She had never heard her father speak about UFOs.

"I think there's something going on there. I mean, it's a perfect location for aliens to visit Earth."

"If there were aliens on the moon, the astronauts would have seen them." She dismissed his argument and moved to one of the seats on the deck and sat down. Her father joined her. It had been years since she had discussions like this with her parents.

"I think they did. Haven't you ever wondered why they stopped going to the moon?"

Keely studied her father. His red hair was mostly gray now. And the twinkle in his blue eyes had gone out. "I thought it had something to do with funding."

"No. That's the BS they fed to the public. I saw a video online where an astronaut spoke to a group and said they had a space force."

"Yes, the president said he was going to start a space force." She recalled a news conference not long ago.

"Keely, this was in the 1960s. We've had a space force for over fifty years now."

Mrs. McGuire brought out some coffee and put it on the coffee table where Keely sat. Her auburn hair was dusted with gray and her green eyes had lost their sparkle as well. When did all this gray hair happen? Why hadn't she noticed before now?

"If we've had a space force for fifty years, why haven't we been told?" Keely asked. She stirred some cream into her coffee. This conversation was getting interesting, but it started a nervous twitch in her stomach.

"It's a matter of national security," her mother said. She sat across the table from Keely and her father. "The government wouldn't want widespread panic."

"The government has denied the alien landings since Roswell and then reversed themselves by feeding us disinformation for years," her father said.

"Why are you two suddenly interested in UFOs?" Keely sipped her coffee.

"Because we've seen one," her mother said.

VAEDRA SYSTEM, PLANET VESTRA MAJOR

INSIDE THE COUNCIL OF NATIONS BUILDING

*L*ieutenant Tremol stood before the small group gathered around the table in Vestra Major's Councilor office. The circular room with large windows sat atop the Capital City's largest building. The view of Sentinel City was breathtaking.

Wearing the dress white unicrin of the Interplanetary Space Patrol, or I.S.P., Tremol cleared his throat.

"Gentlemen, thank you for coming on such short notice."

"Why are we here?" Admiral Esrith demanded. He, too, wore the dress whites, but those of the space military.

"I've come to ask for your participation on a goodwill mission to Earth." He paused to let that sink in and hopefully gain interest.

"Earth?" Councilor Thebes of Vestra Major asked.

"Yes. Earth is a planet in another system that we in the Vaedra System have used for centuries to relocate our people of mixed races."

"Yes, I know what Earth is," Thebes interjected. "What goodwill mission are you talking about?"

Tremol turned to Adam Davis, who sat beside him at the

table. "Adam?" The Earthen who had been mistaken for the criminal, Dram, had become a friend. He hoped Adam could win them over. After all, this was Adam's idea. The group was already showing some interest.

Adam stood, and Tremol sat down.

"When I was abducted and taken to your system, I realized how far advanced your people are compared to us on Earth. I was hoping to get your government to send some ambassadors to our government on Earth and share technology. We could share what we have with you as well." Adam glanced around the table.

"Why should we do that?" Admiral Esrith asked.

"Earth would be a great ally in times of war," Adam said.

"We haven't had a war in decades, thanks to our military," Esrith answered. "We do fine on our own."

"Allies are great in times of war or peace." Tremol stood.

Esrith was going to be a tough sell. He patted Adam on the back.

"There is more information that we could exchange with the people of Earth, not just military prowess. Think of the science or medicine we could exchange." Tremol noticed some councilors perk up.

"I think it's an excellent idea," Councilor Contor of Tarsius said. "It could open up all sorts of trade business for every planet."

Councilor Tal of Persus chimed in, "We could trade our precious metals from our mountains."

"Perhaps the Earthens would trade with us for our silk," Councilor Shim of Vestra Minor added.

"This is great! Does that mean you'll come to Earth?" Adam asked, glancing around the room.

"I need your vote of approval to move forward on this mission. I've already cleared it with my supervisors of the I.S.P." Tremol explained.

"What has the Interplanetary Space Patrol got to do with a goodwill mission to Earth?" Esrith asked.

"As you know, Admiral, the I.S.P. is the first line of defense in our system for law and order. If things escalate, then we call in the military. Sharing this with the Earthens would be essential for them to move to a space-capable military if they don't already have one."

"Are you getting a promotion out of this?" Esrith asked, crossing his arms over his chest.

Tremol tensed his jaw. He knew this was coming. "If all goes well, I hope to get a promotion, yes. But this would elevate all the planets in their standing as far as trade goes. Wouldn't all of the planets benefit from more trade?"

"Yes! We could all use more business. Count the Tarsians in," Contor said, standing.

Tal stood. "Count Persus in as well."

Everyone stood, and the chatter grew louder. Tremol reached across the table and shook hands with many of the councilors, and he shook Adam's hand as well. He felt triumphant at last.

Esrith stood before Tremol, his hat in hand.

Tremol's heart sank. If anyone could put a damper on this mission, it was Admiral Esrith.

"Your father and I go back many years as friends, Tremol. He was a good man. While your idea has merit, you'll have to clear the military's participation with the entire Council, since they oversee the budget for the military. You have my vote if that means anything." Esrith offered his hand and Tremol shook it heartily. This was a surprise. It seemed all his preparation and meetings had paid off. Could this be a turning point in his life and career?

EARTH
VIRGINIA COUNTRYSIDE

"What do you mean, you've seen one?" Keely straightened in her seat, spilling her coffee on the table. Her pulse kicked up a notch and the twitch in her stomach grew.

Her mother sopped up the mess with her napkin as she explained. "We were driving down our road one night when a ship flew over our car and paced us all the way home."

The desolate road that led to her parents' home had no street lights and no other homes since it was farmland on either side for miles.

"What happened when you got home?" The twitch became a knot.

"The ship disappeared," her father said. There was no emotion in his voice.

"If you were any other couple, I would dismiss this as a great figment of your imagination." Keely set her cup down. Both her parents had been in law enforcement for more than twenty years. Now retired, they had time to travel and do things they had always wanted to do. They were trained to observe their surroundings and be able to recall what they had witnessed.

"Have you told anyone about this?"

"No, just you," her mother said, a worried look on her face.

Keely felt helpless. What could she do to help her parents? Who would she confide in? She had no friends or nearby relatives.

"Have they been back?"

Both her parents looked at each other as if deciding whether or not to share their secret.

VESTRA MAJOR

MILITARY COMMITTEE, COUNCIL OF NATIONS BUILDING

The Military Committee was larger than the small delegation Tremol had met with earlier. They were on a different floor of the same building, without the great view. Again, he wore his dress whites to impress the committee. The Chairman pounded his gavel for order and the room grew quiet.

At the front of the room were the Chairman and a councilor on either side of him, sitting at a rectangular table. Everyone else sat in rows of theater seats before them.

"We have a guest today to speak on an urgent matter before we discuss our findings," the Chairman announced. He motioned for Tremol to stand.

"Thank you, Chairman." He turned to face the group of committee members. "I have spoken to several councilors about escorting a small delegation to another system to establish trade relations and exchange technology with the people of Earth. I ask for your support by sending a military ship to escort this delegation to its destination and back."

One of the councilors raised his hand.

"Yes, Councilor Yo from Vestra Minor," the Chairman acknowledged.

"Why should we spend our kashis on this endeavor?"

"Everyone would benefit with opening trade with another system," Tremol began. "Just think of the possibilities for our industries on each of our planets."

Another councilor raised his hand.

"Yes, Councilor Begas from Chroma," the Chairman acknowledged.

"I don't understand why a military ship must be used."

"While we have ventured to the Earth's system in the past with large cargo transports, this will be a larger delegation with scientists, medical professionals, and our military experts," Tremol explained. "We want to explain our technology and show our military capabilities. We hope to, perhaps, train their people in our weapons and flight systems. If we go prepared for more than what they expect, we may only need to do this once."

"I have a question," the Chairman said.

"Yes, sir."

"Won't this leave us vulnerable here in the Vaedra System?"

"Not at all," he began. "In fact, our military has a fleet of ships on standby for each planet, should we have any more problems with the grays. The Interplanetary Space Patrol has immediate jurisdiction of the space between the planets, and the military covers beyond that."

Admiral Esrith stood. "May I add that we have not had any problems with the grays for decades, but we continue to monitor the space around the Zeta Reticulin system. We have the capability to destroy a planet and the grays know this. You can rest assured that the Vaedra System is in good hands with one battleship out of the equation."

The room remained silent for a moment until the Chairman banged his gavel. "If there are no more questions, we will have a discussion and then vote. Steward, will you escort these gentlemen out for now?"

Another man approached Tremol and he followed him to where Admiral Esrith stood. Then the three of them left the meeting room.

Tremol noticed a lounge with a couple people placing orders at the counter. He needed a drink and an excuse to get away from Admiral Esrith.

"This may take a while, Admiral," he said, trying to excuse himself.

"I'll buy you a drink, Tremol," the admiral said.

He was taken aback. "You're on." Why would Esrith do that? They walked toward the lounge.

"Two detonators, please," Admiral Esrith said and handed the bartender some kashis to cover the drinks.

Detonators were strong drinks. What was the admiral up to?

"I've spoken to Command at the I.S.P.," Esrith began.

He raised his glass. "Oh?"

"It seems they have a bet going." Esrith took a sip of his drink.

He sipped his drink, too, and a bad feeling swept over him. He swallowed hard.

"They're betting that you don't succeed with this mission."

"So why are you interested in this venture?"

"Let's say I like the odds."

"So, you bet against me as well?"

"On the contrary. I'm betting that you succeed."

"Why would my own people bet against me?"

"I'd say they have information they failed to give you when you first approached them."

"And would you be willing to share this information?"

He glanced at the admiral then swallowed the last of his drink.

Admiral Esrith downed the last of his drink and leaned closer.

"What position were you aspiring to if you succeed?"

"Commander."

"Ahh. I suppose you'll be in charge of the new Special Missions group, then?"

"That's my hope, sir."

"And what price are you willing to pay for this information?"

"I will not compromise my ethics or values." He stood, ready to leave but the admiral grabbed his arm.

"That's the answer I was looking for."

EARTH
VIRGINIA COUNTRYSIDE

"What aren't you telling me?" Keely jumped up from her seat, her hands on her hips, heart pounding. The cool breeze made her shiver in her light cotton t-shirt. She looked at both her parents sitting opposite each other at the coffee table.

"We aren't sure," her father began, "but we woke up in our bed the next day and neither one of us could remember anything after we got out of the car."

Keely's mouth dropped open. "Have you seen a doctor?"

"As a matter of fact, we both have appointments to have MRIs done this week," her mother said.

"You suspect something, don't you?" Keely asked, worry setting in. She sat back down in her seat.

Her parents looked at each other. "I found a knot in my leg not too long after the incident," her father said. He leaned toward her and rolled up his pant leg to show her the spot.

"And I've been having headaches. I've even heard voices in my head," her mother said.

"And I've been having nightmares," her father added.

"And just look at our hair," her mother said. "We've gone gray overnight."

"I wondered about that. And you've told no one about this?"

"Who would believe us?" her father asked, leaning back in his seat. He put his arm over the back of the chair.

"I believe you." Keely leaned forward in her seat, crossing her legs. Her nerves getting the most of her, she rocked her top leg back and forth as she clenched her jaw. She noticed how similar her coloring was to her mother's, along with the freckles the three of them shared. Her father was even paler than her and her mother. "I'll ask around and see if there is someone monitoring this kind of activity," she offered. Certainly, someone in the government would know about this. But could they do anything about it?

"We've been doing some research online," her father said. He leaned forward again, his hands on his knees.

"What kind of research?"

"Well, I know it sounds like a conspiracy, but I...we... believe it has something to do with the grays. Apparently, they have been abducting people all over the planet."

"Yes, and not just once," her mother added.

"What do you mean?" Keely held her breath, the knot in her stomach tightened.

"It seems they like to re-visit those they've experimented on and do more experiments."

THE CONCORDANCE

HYPERSPACE

*S*itting in the main deck and strapped in for hyperspace flight, Tremol reflected on the bet the I.S.P. had against his mission and the events that got him this far. Why give him permission to go and with all this funding if they didn't think he could do it? He had gone to the I.S.P. first because Adam had the idea and *he* had the connections. If they didn't want him to lead it, the I.S.P. could have assigned someone else. It was his idea about the promotion. Why go through all this trouble if he couldn't better himself? This would prove that he was capable of leading and organizing. Those were at least two of the traits for a commander.

The pressure against his body held him firmly in place, but he was able to glance sideways at Adam Davis, who sat beside him. Adam wore a t-shirt and jeans, as he called them, with I.S.P.-issued boots, since all Adam had were the rubber boots he'd left Earth wearing. *He* wore his I.S.P. flight suit.

He had met Adam a few moon cycles ago when Adam was able to convince the I.S.P. to help rescue Genesis and thirty slave girls. He wanted to hate Adam for suggesting the subsequent missions, but a lot of the agents ended up with promotions after capturing the slave-trader, Dram, including himself.

Now, here they were, in the Concordance, a Class A Star Destroyer, carrying scientists, medical professionals, pilots, Admiral Esrith and his crew, along with two councilors, who, with the full authority of the Nations, could speak for them in this matter.

Everything was working out so far. So, what did the I.S.P. know that would prevent his success? And why wouldn't they share that information with him?

Admiral Esrith set their destination to arrive near Mars, as Adam had pointed out on the cosmic maps.

"Coming out of hyperspace, Admiral," the ensign announced.

"What the hell?" Adam said.

Tremol looked out the viewport. Beside the larger moon, a battleship hovered in space with the letters USA emblazoned on the port side. There were at least two smaller vessels near the larger one.

A flash of light came from the larger ship. Moments later, a boom sounded, rocking and shaking the bridge.

"Shields up!" the admiral called out. He turned to Adam. "Does your government have a space-capable military?"

"Uh, not that I know of. But those are the initials of my country." Adam pointed to the larger ship.

Another flash and boom rocked the ship, but the shields held off the damage. "Take evasive action!" the admiral called out.

"We're not going to fire back, Admiral?" the ensign asked.

"No. We don't want to start a war. This is a peaceful mission. Most likely we surprised them. Stay on course for Earth."

Tremol watched from his seat as the ensign called out the navigator's coordinates. His gut told him something didn't feel right. The helmsman pushed the throttle forward and they took off. The next destination was Earth's moon.

He glanced at Adam, but Adam spoke to Genesis. If only Genesis had chosen *him* to be her mate instead of Adam, things would be different. He had known her since she was fourteen anos. Genesis had grown and matured into a beautiful, headstrong woman, something he admired. But because of all the time he spent in training, he lost any chance of finding a mate. Adam didn't know how lucky he really was. And was he holding back information? Who were those people who shot at them? Is that what the admiral alluded to in the bet?

EARTH

WASHINGTON, D.C.

*M*onday morning, Keely headed to the White House in her Chrysler Sebring convertible with the top down, chewing her bottom lip. She loved the feel of the wind through her hair but today, she wore it pulled back in a tight bun, still wet from her shower. She wore the antique poison ring David had given her recently. It was the only jewelry she had, other than the watch and diamond stud earrings her parents had given her when she became a Secret Service agent.

She had meant to tell her parents about her second thoughts on the Secret Service. She'd worked very hard to get where she was but there was a nagging feeling in her gut that she was out of her league. How could she say that to her parents after what they had just been through? And David, he wouldn't understand either. Besides, she wasn't about to tell him who she worked for. With all her training and college, she hadn't had time for a personal life. David just happened to be the first man who gave her any attention.

But the thoughts of the weekend visit with her parents still haunted her. Where would she start her research? Who could she ask about UFOs? What agency monitored that kind of behavior?

Her parents' appointment for MRIs was not until Tuesday. The wait would be unbearable.

THE CONCORDANCE
EARTH'S MOON

*L*ater, as the Concordance came up to Earth's moon, Adam unleashed his harness, stood up, and walked toward the viewport.

"This is unbelievable!"

Tremol removed his harness as well and moved to Adam's left. Genesis joined them, moving to Adam's right.

"What is it?" he asked.

"That's the dark side of the moon. There's a colony there!"

"It looks like a city of some sort," Tremol said.

"Yes! We were all led to believe there was no life on the moon, nothing but rocks."

"Someone lied," he said. He glanced at Adam.

"Exactly!"

The Navigator searched for the coordinates for Adam's ultimate destination, while he, Adam and Genesis returned to their seats.

"How could your government betray you like that?" he asked.

"They betrayed everyone. I thought what I had heard

were conspiracy theories, but this...this is real. And to top it off, they covered up everything."

"Do you still want to continue the mission?" he found himself asking. If Adam said no, he would return a failure, just like the I.S.P. figured.

"I, uh, have a favor to ask of you, Tremol," Adam said to him in a whisper.

"What is it?"

"I have a feeling that something isn't right."

"I feel it, too. Did you have a premonition?" Adam's premonitions proved to be accurate in the past. He made the mistake of not believing in him once and he wouldn't do it again.

"Just flashes of an image."

"What kind of image?"

"A little gray creature with large, black eyes, but that's been a conspiracy theory for years."

"The grays? They are real. Admiral Esrith fought them decades ago. Let me inform him." He turned to leave but Adam grabbed his arm.

"I have a suggestion. Instead of all of us going to NASA in one ship, I think I should go with the councilors. If something happens to me, then I can still speak to Genesis telepathically. You'll be my backup."

"The admiral won't let you fly his ship. He will appoint a pilot to fly you down."

"I'm good with that. I would feel better if you looked after Genesis for me."

"You trust me with her?" He couldn't believe what he heard.

"Of course. I know we've had our differences, but I trust both of you."

"Thank you." Tremol offered his hand to Adam and they shook on it. He couldn't believe the trust Adam bestowed on him. But could he trust himself with her? Alone? Although she turned him down for Adam, she still held his heart. How could he fly with her and not want to touch her or hold her?

Standing in the hangar bay, Tremol, Councilors Thebes and Contor, Adam and Genesis waited for their pilot, while the crew loaded their ship with supplies.

"Ready?" Genesis smiled at Adam, smoothing his t-shirt.

"Yeah, let's get this over with."

"You don't sound as excited as you were before we left. What's wrong?"

"That ship that shot at us from the moon of Mars? I just can't get that out of my head. I don't know how Earth can defend against something like that."

"That's why we're here, right? To help your people get the technology they need so they can be prepared for this type of thing?"

"Yes. Yes, we are." He smiled back at Genesis before pulling her close and giving her a passionate kiss which she returned.

Tremol looked away. He was uncomfortable watching Adam kiss the woman who could have been his mate. He had to stop thinking of her that way. She had made her choice and she was obviously happy.

He noticed Eno, the pilot, approaching and went to pull Genesis away from her mate. He escorted her a safe distance to the viewing platform above the hangar. He gripped the railing hard so as not to put his arm around her. He had to be strong. Adam's trust was important to him and he wouldn't break that trust.

Moments later, Eno, Adam and the councilors climbed into Shadow One.

Adam sat beside Eno in the cockpit, with Councilors Contor and Thebes sitting behind them. This ship was wedge-shaped and had cloaking abilities. A smooth ride, but it handled much differently than Genesis' ship, the Guardian.

Adam tapped in the coordinates for NASA at Kennedy Space Center in Florida as Eno took control of the ship.

"Once we get into the atmosphere, we'll try to contact NASA," Adam said.

SPACE FORCE COMMAND

a room full of computers, monitors, and military men and women watching screens of various areas in space and on Earth.

"No more signs of alien ships near Phobos?" Major Forshen asked the group of men and women.

"Sir, I've got something in the southern quadrant above Earth, moving into our atmosphere. It appears to have the same signature as the ship we shot at from Phobos."

Major Forshen approached the computer. "What is it, specialist?"

"A large object moving into our upper atmosphere near the equator, sir."

He stood behind her and glanced at the object. "Can anyone pick up communications?"

"I think I've got something, sir," another specialist announced, turning up the volume...

11

___

SHADOW ONE

*a*dam looked through the viewport and could see the Florida coastline when a broadcast came across the comms.

"This is NASA, identify yourself."

Adam pressed the comm key. "This is Adam Davis. I'm a resident of Tennessee and I'm with a contingent of people from the Vaedra System on a diplomatic mission."

12

NASA

A man at NASA communications looked up when Adam mentioned Tennessee. "Is he kidding? Did he just say, Tennessee?"

The comms guy nodded. "Yeah. Tennessee. What should I say?"

"Tell him to hold his position and I'll let the Chief know." He raced out of the room.

"This is NASA, hold your position. Do not enter Earth's atmosphere."

Within a minute, the Chief came into the room. "Let me have a headset," he said.

"This is Chief Dallin from NASA. Please identify yourself and state your purpose again?"

"This is Adam Davis. I'm a resident of Tennessee. I was abducted by aliens about two months ago. I'm returning with the people of the Vaedra System. We are on a diplomatic mission. We're requesting permission to land at Kennedy Space Center."

"I don't think we can accommodate your ship."

"We have a smaller ship, sir. Only a few of us will be arriving."

"All right. Permission granted."

Dallin took off his headset. "I want you to monitor this frequency and let me know if there are any more communications."

He turned to his right-hand man. "Get me Yermolay."

13

SPACE FORCE COMMAND

"Get a team down at Kennedy right away," Forshen ordered.

EARTH

WASHINGTON, D.C.

*K*eely removed her poison ring at the checkpoint since the alarm kept going off. The agent picked it up and looked it over, while Keely walked through the scanner.

"It's a poison ring," she explained. Keely took the ring and opened it, showing off the empty chamber inside. "This is where they would put the poison. It's an antique ring." She placed it back on her finger.

"A bit morbid, isn't it?" the agent said.

"I love the colors and the design." Keely admired it as she slipped it back on her finger. She shoved her Sig Sauer back into its holster and straightened her bulletproof vest. Walking to the briefing room, she reminded herself to ask about UFO monitoring, but Tom Gowan, her supervisor, stopped her before she entered.

"I want you to consider stepping up your game, McGuire."

"My game, sir?"

"Yes. Come with me."

She followed Gowan to his office. The knot in her stomach from the day before returned with a vengeance.

Now wasn't the time to ask about UFOs or abduction monitoring.

He turned to speak with her, once they were at the doorway. "I want to know why you don't apply yourself." Gowan stood before her, arms crossed.

"I'm not sure what you mean, sir."

"I think you are capable of doing more, McGuire."

"I'm giving one-hundred percent, sir. Every day."

He shook his head. "I want more from you, McGuire. Do you understand?"

"Yes, sir." She lowered her head. What more could she give? If a hundred percent wasn't good enough, then maybe *she* wasn't good enough?

15

SHADOW ONE

*A*dam pressed the comm-link. "NASA, can you read? This is Adam Davis from Shadow One, can you read?"

"This is NASA. You are cleared for landing at pad 3."

Eno searched visually and pointed to a pad with the number 3 on it. He hovered over the spot momentarily, then set Shadow One on the ground.

"Ready, boys?" Adam asked.

Eno wore the flight suit of Vaedra's Space Military, which was a navy-blue color, where the I.S.P. wore white. The two councilors wore black robes with red trim around the collars, covering a long red tunic and black pants. Each collar had an insignia of the planet and region that they represented. Eno's insignia was impressive as well, with the Space Military logo and a smaller logo signifying his pilot status, but was worn over the heart. Adam felt underdressed.

The two Councilors nodded, then proceeded to the ramp door.

"As the only officer here, I'll stay with the ship," Eno said.

Once the ramp lowered, Adam faced a large group of armed military men with weapons aimed at him and his companions.

His heart skipped a beat at the sight of all the military present. "Whoa! Is that any way to greet a visitor?" He raised his arms over his head. The other two did the same.

A uniformed officer stepped forward. "And who are you?" the officer asked. The man had several stripes on his sleeve and insignias on his uniform front.

"I'm Adam Davis, sir. I was abducted a couple months ago and taken to the Vaedra System. I convinced these two councilors to come back with me to talk about sharing technology with Earth.

"Check them for weapons," the officer ordered. "And see if there are any others aboard the ship."

Four military men approached them and patted them down. Two others boarded the ship.

"We found a pilot aboard ship, sir," one of the men said, coming down the ramp. The other man followed behind Eno with his weapon drawn.

"What's this?" One of the military men asked about Eno's black box.

"That's my scanner," Eno replied.

"What is its purpose?" the officer asked.

"To close and open the ship, among other things," Eno said.

"I'll take care of that for you," the officer replied. His weapon aimed at Eno's chest.

Eno reluctantly relinquished the scanner.

Once the pat-down was finished, the officer ordered them brought to a room for interrogation. He whispered something to one of the men and handed him Eno's scanner.

The four of them were escorted with a man on either

side of each of them, followed by several more men with weapons. One man led them inside a small office where they each took a seat facing the only desk in the room. All the men left but one. "The general will be in to speak to you shortly," he said, then he too left.

"Is this normal protocol for visitors from other galaxies?" Contor asked.

"I'm not sure, sir. I've never come back from an abduction under these circumstances," Adam replied.

"You've been back, then?" Thebes asked.

"Yes. Genesis returned me to my home, but I realized almost too late that I loved her, so I went back with her to Atria. This is my second return," Adam said, "but I assure you, I had no idea this would happen. It's my first time being at NASA."

"I hope they don't try to take apart my scanner. I won't be able to get the ramp open again if they do," Eno added.

"That could be a problem," Adam said.

The door opened, and another officer entered with even more insignias and stripes then the last one. He was accompanied by a couple of armed soldiers.

"Good afternoon, gentlemen," he announced, then sat at the desk. "What can I do for you?"

"First of all, you can return Eno's scanner," Adam said.

"Now, why would I want to do that?" the general asked.

"Because it doesn't belong to you and we came here in good faith, as a diplomatic mission, to share technology with you and exchange scientific and engineering information for studying," he answered.

"What makes you think we need their technology?" the general asked, looking at each of them.

"Because we don't have tech like they have," Adam responded.

"How do you know we don't?"

"I think the general has already worked something out with another group of aliens," Contor said aloud.

The general smirked at that. "How astute. And where do you hail from?"

"We are both councilors from the Vaedra System and we came here to not only exchange technology but to open trade between our two systems. May we speak to your leader?"

"*I* am the leader here, and the only one you will be speaking with," he said.

"You aren't the leader!" Adam stood and pointed at the general. He turned and faced his friends. "We have a President of the United States and he's the one we will be speaking to." He turned to face the general once again. "I demand to speak to the President." He curled his hands into fists.

"You can demand all you want but you won't get it. The President is a very busy man. He has people like me to deal with alien threats."

"We're not a threat. We're here on a diplomatic mission. We need to speak to the President," Contor said.

Adam sat back in his seat.

"Didn't you say you have the same technology as we do?" Eno asked.

"Yes," the general said.

"Then you must know what we are capable of if we don't see this President," Eno said.

"Now, that sounded like a threat to me," the general said.

"The real question is, which alien group are you dealing with, General?" Thebes asked.

THE WHITE HOUSE
WASHINGTON, D.C.

*K*eely's assignment was always in uniformed protection and today she stood watch outside the Cabinet room where the secretaries met.

How was she supposed to up her game? The day slipped by uneventfully, but the thought of Gowan's message bothered her. On top of that, her parents' recent experience with aliens gnawed at her. She twisted the poison ring on her finger and thought of David.

She met him at a party where she tried to fit in with the Washington crowd. Most of the agents she knew treated her like one of the boys. Wasn't that what she wanted? No one ever asked her out except David. He treated her as if she was special and she liked that, but what did she really know about him? All she knew was he lived in D.C. and wrote for a local paper. Sure, he asked her a lot of questions, but he rarely opened up about himself. Even her mother thought he was too good to be true.

"Escort the Cabinet members to the elevator," her supervisor announced in her earbuds.

She opened the door to allow them to enter the hall and escorted them, as she was told. She allowed so many on the elevator at a time and then controlled the panel until everyone was down.

When her shift ended, she headed home to do some research. Her phone rang as she entered her apartment.

"Hello, David." She tossed her keys on the desk. Her heart lightened at his voice.

"We've got to talk."

"I'm home now, did you want to come over?" This sounded serious.

"No. I'm calling to let you know I'll be out of town for a little while. I've got an assignment in Turkey."

"Turkey? What will you be doing there?" Her heart dropped at his words.

"I can't talk about it. I'll fill you in when I return."

"Oh. When will you be back?"

"I'm not sure, but I'll call you when I return."

"Okay. Make sure that you do, and be safe."

That was odd. She had seen him twice last week before visiting her parents and he didn't say anything about traveling. She set her phone on the bar and played with the ring on her finger.

She opened her laptop and booted it up while fixing herself something to eat. Then she sat at the desk and typed in "government agencies that deal with alien abductions".

A lot of things popped up on the screen. She clicked on the first one, "Alien Abduction." It basically told her parents' story, while others were abducted from their beds, homes, cars and other places. It mentioned that the abductees were subjected to experiments of a violent, sexual nature. They often reported "missing time" and having no memories of the events. Only under hypnosis were the recollections retrieved.

She clicked on the video that was with the article and her heart rate increased when she learned that abductions occurred in almost six percent of the population. The grays were the abductors and they spoke telepathically to all their abductees.

The video went on to suggest that some of these abductions could be caused by demonization. In some cases, calling on the name of Jesus made the experience go away, but not in all cases.

She went to the next article, "UFOs: Fact or Fiction?", which showed the CIA page. It stated that the collection of information by the CIA was from the 1940s through the 1990s.

She clicked on the link, "CIA's Role in the Study of UFOs," but it didn't show any articles on them. She went back to the original page and started looking at the documents there. There were at least nine pages with several documents on each page. This was going to be a long night.

THE CONCORDANCE, ABOVE EARTH ATMOSPHERE

*T*remol paced back and forth on the bridge. How could this happen? The four of them were gone too long. The I.S.P. would love to see him fail.

"We should have gotten word of something since the landing," Admiral Esrith said.

"That's what concerns me." He stopped pacing. "Was there any information from the I.S.P. that would alert you to this event?"

"No. Just that they had a bet. They didn't elaborate further, but I have some thoughts on the matter."

"Oh? Care to share that?"

"I'll wait. I don't want to assume anything just yet."

"Well, Adam had a premonition of sorts."

"A premonition? Is he subject to having them often?"

"Yes, and every one he has had has come true."

"Well?"

"He's seen images of the grays."

"I knew it!"

Genesis closed her eyes and tried to contact Adam mentally.

"They are being interrogated," Genesis said.

"How do you know this?" Esrith asked.

"She's a telepath," Tremol said.

"And Adam, too?"

"Only with me," Genesis said.

"Get Shadow Two ready," Admiral Esrith ordered. "Oh, and add that extra equipment we brought for surveillance and rescue."

"Aye, Admiral," Captain Melbus replied.

NASA/KENNEDY SPACE CENTER

"Tell me, General, have you been working with the grays?" Contor asked.

The general glared at Contor. "Why do you ask?"

"General, I hope you have listened to the Pleiadians," Thebes said.

"We have been in touch with both groups."

Adam glanced at both the councilors, then the general.

"Pleiadians?" Adam asked.

"The Pleiadians are descendants of the Lyrans who have had a large part in the history of many of the inhabited planets throughout the universe. Humans are descendants of a race of Lyrans," Thebes said.

"Yes, the Pleiadians have a highly developed spiritual knowledge that enables them to use certain spiritual powers such as healing, telepathy and telekinesis." Contor added.

"Much like we do on our planets," Thebes said.

"What about the grays?" Adam asked.

Thebes looked directly at the general. "The grays are not to be trusted. They are extraterrestrial biological entities. They are not human."

"We've banned them from the Vaedra System," Contor

added. "They like to experiment on humans and we won't allow it."

"Your star system may have undergone similar growth under the Lyrans as did the Vaedra System," Thebes added.

The general stood up. "Gentlemen, I will return."

He walked to the door and his two guards left with him. In a couple minutes, smoke streamed through the air vents.

Adam jumped up and ran to the door. Locked.

"Genesis, we're locked in a room with some kind of gas pouring through the vents. Go to plan B."

THE CONCORDANCE

Genesis relayed the message.

Tremol headed for Shadow Two with long strides while Genesis trotted behind him.

"Why did this have to happen on my watch?" he mumbled.

He performed the pre-flight sequence without waiting for Genesis.

"I'm here, remember? I can help you with that."

He had too much on his mind to answer her. He piloted the Shadow Two down into Earth's atmosphere. The wedge-shaped ship allowed for faster travel.

Genesis reached for the cloaking shields.

"What are you doing?" He glanced at her.

"I'm cloaking the ship. We don't need any more trouble."

Maybe that was a good idea, but he wouldn't tell her that.

She gave him the coordinates for Adam's former boss, Jeremy Smith's home.

"Why do we need this person?" he asked.

"He knows this Earth better than us. He can help."

Once they landed in front of Smith's dwelling, Genesis

lowered the ramp of the ship. "I've met him before. Let me approach first," she said. She handed him the scanner.

They climbed the steps of a log cabin. Genesis listened for sounds. "Anyone there?" she called out.

The door opened and a woman stood at the entrance. "Can I help you?" she asked. She looked them both over through a crack in the door.

"I am looking for Jeremy Smith. I am Genesis, the mate of Adam Davis."

"Jeremy!" the woman called out. He appeared behind her.

"Hey! You're back. Where's Adam?" He craned his neck to look out the door.

Tremol took a step up onto the porch.

"We need your assistance. Adam met with your people at NASA and after being interrogated, his captors gassed them all," Genesis said.

"Good Lord," Jeremy said.

"Adam was with two of our councilors and a pilot. They are all believed to be in danger. We are here on a diplomatic mission. It is imperative that you come with us," he said.

"And who are you?" Jeremy asked him.

"This is Lieutenant Tremol of the Interplanetary Space Patrol. He is in charge of this mission," Genesis added.

"Uh, Misty, I'll be back," Jeremy said.

"When?"

"What?"

"When will you be back? This doesn't sound like it'll be in a few minutes."

"Hell, I don't know. When we find Adam. I've got my phone. I'll call you."

Misty hugged him fiercely and he gave her a kiss. He and Genesis stepped off the porch and headed for the cloaked ship.

"Hey guys, what are we traveling in?"

Tremol hit the controls on the scanner and the ramp opened.

"Damn! It's cloaked. How cool is that?" Jeremy said.

Tremol went up the ramp first. Genesis followed with Jeremy. He took his position in the pilot's seat, while Genesis showed Jeremy where to sit. "Strap in," she said, then sat in the co-pilot's seat.

Within minutes, they flew over Washington, D.C. He didn't know how, but he hoped this other Earthen could help convince the President of this mission. He listened while Genesis filled Jeremy in on what had happened so far.

"There! That's the White House," Jeremy said. "How are we going to get in there? That place is well guarded."

"We're still cloaked. Landing shouldn't be a problem," Tremol said.

20

NASA

"*D*allin?" Major Sinclair barked to the room full of NASA workers.

An employee pointed to a door down the hall.

Sinclair knocked before pushing the door open. Dallin stood up. "Who are you?"

"Major Sinclair of the U.S. Space Force. I'm here to retrieve our extraterrestrial guests."

"What guests?"

"We intercepted your communications with another craft. We know they landed here. You *will* turn them over to us at once."

21

WASHINGTON, D.C

*E*xhausted after researching until late the night before, Keely called her mother early in the morning, to check in.

"Hi, Mom, how are you?" Keely asked, holding her cell phone up to her ear with her shoulder. She used the spatula to retrieve her eggs before they burned. Setting them on her plate, she grabbed her phone with her hand and set the plate of food on her bar table.

Listening to her mother's tale of what was going on around the countryside, she scarfed down her breakfast. She got two gulps of coffee down before her mother asked the question she dreaded.

"How's David? Anything serious going on?"

"No, but he will be out of town for a while."

"I never liked that guy."

"You never met him, Mom."

"I know, but he's too...mysterious, you know?"

She hadn't thought of him in those terms, but it was true. She didn't know much about him at all.

"I called to see if you and dad had your MRIs yet?"

"We go in this afternoon."

"Be sure to call me later. I want to know what the doctor thinks." She hesitated about telling her mother about the research. But they had done research as well and probably already knew what she just found last night.

"Will do."

"Love you, Mom."

"Love you, too, baby."

Her research didn't pull up any helpful information. It just proved how secretive the government really was with its own citizens and that was unfortunate. It would take someone on the inside to dig a little deeper and she didn't know who would be willing to help. Knowing this was going on was one thing, but what do you do about it after the fact? No wonder abductees didn't talk about this except with other abductees.

Dressed in her uniform, vest and working shoes, she entered the White House and went through proper protocol. Again, the buzzer went off as she was scanned for weapons and contraband. She had already placed her Sig on the table. She removed her watch and it went off again.

"Got any other jewelry?" The agent looked at her hand.

She glanced down. "Oh, I forgot my ring." She wedged it off her finger and handed it to the agent.

The agent ran the scanner over her and it didn't buzz this time. He gingerly handed the ring back to her.

Keely picked up her other possessions. She shoved her ring on and slipped her weapon into its holster. Refastening her watch, she reached her supervisor, Tom Gowan. He briefed her on the previous day and what was planned for today. She put in her earbuds and clipped on her radio, then looked over the day's schedule.

She stood at attention in the hall outside the President's

Oval office. She hoped she could stay awake for her entire shift as she stifled a yawn.

"Coffee service, coming through," she heard in her earpiece.

When the aide approached her, she set the tray of coffee and accoutrements down on a nearby table. Keely did a pat-down on the aide while another agent ran a wand back to front over the aide.

"You're good to go," Keely said, opening the door for the woman. She stepped inside, holding the door as the aide set the tray on a table facing the windows behind the desk. The President sat on one of the sofas.

A sudden movement outside the window caught her attention. Her pulse shot up a notch. It looked like a ramp opened on the lawn, coming out of an invisible object. She spoke into her headset.

"We've got movement on the lawn, outside the Oval office. It appears to be three individuals. Two in white jump-suits, one in blue jeans and a black t-shirt," she reported.

The aide froze with the tray, staring out the window at the commotion. Keely could see a couple of Secret Service agents running toward them when suddenly they both fell on their backs. The three individuals stood in front of the window, staring back at her and the aide.

She received a transmission from Gowan.

"I need you outside! Stat!"

Keely rushed down the hall, wide awake now, adrenaline pumping through her veins. She reached Gowan's office and hesitated.

"Handle it!" he shouted.

She continued out the door and joined Agent Smith and another agent as they turned toward the suspects.

22

WHITE HOUSE LAWN

*H*er heart pounded. *Please God, help me,* she prayed. Relief trickled over her when she joined the other two agents. Seeing she wasn't alone gave her more courage.

She pulled her weapon from its holster. One agent raced to check on the two downed agents while she and Agent Smith hugged the building toward the three suspects on the front lawn.

"Keep to the building," she whispered to Smith. "I think there is something in the lawn we can't see."

The three people standing in front of the President's window turned when she spoke.

Great. "Hands up!" she shouted.

The man in blue jeans did as he was told. The two dressed in white jumpsuits hesitated, then followed suit.

"What is your business here?" she asked, her Sig pointed at the taller man in white.

"We're here to see the President," the man in jeans responded. "It's a matter of national security."

"We'll see about that," Agent Smith said. "Pat them down, I'll cover."

"Me?" Her heart skipped a beat. *I can do this. I'm trained for this.* She started with the man in blue jeans, after holstering her weapon. He had a pocket knife and a couple of coins in his one front pocket and a cell phone in the other. He had a wallet in his back pocket. Keely removed everything and put it in her pocket. She moved on to the woman. She had nothing, not even pockets, and as far as she could figure out, she went commando all the way. All except a black box, which Keely removed from the woman's shoulder. When she got to the big guy, her heart skipped another beat. He was incredibly handsome, with dark brownish-black hair and brown eyes. Penetrating eyes that wouldn't leave her. He, too, went commando. That was odd for someone wearing white. While she came up the other side, he whispered in her ear.

"If this is a search for weapons, you're not doing it correctly."

The sound of his voice sent a wave of emotions through her. "I'm not doing it correctly? So, you have experience in searching people?"

"Yes, I do, and you're not doing it correctly."

"Do you have contraband we should know about?" she asked.

"I don't know what you mean by that?"

"Contraband. Illegal stuff?" She put her hands on her hips.

His stare became intense. "We are here on a diplomatic mission from Vaedra."

She pulled her Sig Sauer out and pointed it at the tall man.

"Move it, big guy."

Smith escorted the trio to Tom Gowan, who checked them again for weapons and collected the black box and pocket items from Keely, along with the cell phone. The tall man's eyes bore into her, making her uncomfortable.

"Have a seat," Gowan instructed them.

After the trio sat, Gowan escorted the woman into another room for interrogation. Keely and Agent Smith each guarded a door, awaiting further instructions. Her heart rate calmed a little.

"Are you from the Huanti clans?" the handsome one asked her.

"What did you say?"

The man in jeans followed the conversation. "The Huanti clans all have blue eyes and orange hair and live on Plexus."

Agent Smith stifled a smile.

"I've never heard of Plexus. Where is it?" *Is this guy for real?*

"It's in the farthest quadrant of the Vaedra System."

"The Vaedra System? What is that?"

The man in jeans chuckled. "This is Lieutenant Tremol of the Interplanetary Space Patrol. He's here escorting a group of dignitaries from the Vaedra System on a diplomatic mission."

"Very good," Tremol glanced at the man in jeans.

"See, I was listening."

"And this is Jeremy Smith, a contractor from Tennessee who is a friend of Adam Davis, one of those on the mission," Tremol said, gesturing to the man in jeans.

Jeremy nodded.

"And how do you two know each other?" Agent Smith asked.

"Adam was abducted by Genesis a couple months ago," Jeremy began. "When she brought him back to Earth he decided to return with her because he loved her. He vowed to come back after helping her find her parents.

Adam used to work for me, building log cabins in the Smokies."

"Yes, and I was assigned to escort a small group of councilors, scientists, medical professionals, Adam and Genesis to speak to Adam's leaders about sharing technology and opening trade relations."

"So, where are the others?" she asked. *This story sounds off.*

"That's exactly what we are here to find out," he responded.

The door opened and Genesis and Gowan stepped out.

"Next?"

Tremol stood and followed the supervisor inside the room.

"And your function here?" Agent Smith looked at Jeremy.

"I'm here to translate, so to speak, and I've met Genesis once before. We really need to see the President." He leaned forward in the seat.

A few minutes later, Tremol returned and Jeremy went inside to speak to Gowan.

"Can you get us an audience with your leader?" Tremol asked Keely, standing too close for comfort. She craned her neck to look up into those brown eyes of his.

"You just spoke to my supervisor."

"I mean the leader of your planet."

Keely glanced over at Agent Smith. *He's got to be kidding.*

"We don't have a leader of the planet. Only leaders of countries," Agent Smith clarified.

"What country is Vaedra in?" she asked.

"Vaedra is another star system just beyond Andromeda. Do you know Andromeda?"

Her heart pounded again. She read about that last night. This guy was talking as if he was...

"Wait." She pushed him back a little. "Are you telling me you're an alien?"

His penetrating gaze made it hard to think.

"To you, yes."

She squeezed both his arms. "You feel real."

"I assure you, I am. Are you all right?"

She shook her head. *This isn't happening*, she thought. Her parents had just been abducted and now she was meeting aliens at the White House? She rubbed her head with both hands.

Genesis tapped her headband, then spoke to Tremol in another language and he replied in that language.

"Speak English, please," Keely said, then realized they'd missed the woman's headband. The tall man looked amused by all this.

She walked over to the woman called Genesis and reached for her headband. "What is this?"

"It is my translator." She took it off and placed it on Keely's forehead.

"Tannae se ut!" Genesis said.

She heard, "Hold it there!"

The door to the interrogation room opened and Jeremy and Tom Gowan walked out.

"McGuire, Smith." Their supervisor gestured for them to approach.

She handed Genesis the translator and walked over to Gowan. The tall man slowly moved out of her way.

"Yes, sir," McGuire and Smith replied simultaneously.

"We will treat this as a highly sensitive matter. I will go in and brief the President and McGuire will be in charge of our guests."

"In charge, sir?" She swallowed hard. "What exactly does that entail?" she asked.

"We'll leave that up to the President."

Her hands began to sweat.

Gowan turned and headed toward the President's office.

Keely and Smith stood watch, awaiting word from their supervisor.

"Your name is McGuire?" the tall man asked.

She nodded. *This guy may be a problem.*

"McGuire, you may escort our visitors to the President's Oval Office," Gowan announced through her earpiece.

"You're up," Agent Smith gestured to her.

"This way, please," she said to the guests and led them to the President's office.

Once inside, Gowan stood off to one side, while Keely introduced the three visitors the best she could. The whole thing felt surreal to her.

"Mr. President," Tremol began, "We are visiting from the Vaedra System on the behest of Adam Davis, who wanted us to share our technology with your planet. He suggested that our system and your planet may want to open trade negotiations that would benefit both of us."

"That sounds like a great idea," the President responded. "I'll call a meeting of the Cabinet to get the ball rolling."

Genesis held up her hand. "There is a slight problem, Mr. President."

"Oh? What is that?"

Tremol stepped forward, interrupting Genesis. "Our landing party, which consists of a pilot, Adam Davis, and Councilors Thebes and Contor, are not responding to our hails. They landed at your NASA base in Florida over six hours ago."

Genesis glanced up at Tremol with a scowl on her face.

"Yes, and I am a healer and telepath and can speak to Adam, who is also my mate," Genesis explained. "The last time I heard from him, they were taken to a room for interrogation and then a gas emitting from the vents silenced them all."

"I was part of plan B," Jeremy added. "Adam worked for me in my log cabin business. I can vouch for what they're telling you." He reached into his pocket and pulled out the gold coin, which had been returned to him when he was interrogated. He handed it to the President.

"Adam helped capture a slave-trader on Vaedra and was paid this gold for his reward. I had it checked out. It's purer than any gold found on Earth. Adam asked me to pay off his mortgage with it. You can have your scientists check it out if you don't believe any of it."

"Oh, I believe you. So, you think the group is being held at NASA?" the President asked.

"Yes." Genesis added.

"Can you get your people on this? Find out what's happened to their landing party?" the President asked Gowan.

"We're on it sir," he said.

23

SECRET UNDERWATER BASE
PACIFIC OCEAN

*E*no awoke alone in a small room with a bunk bed and a type of cleansing compartment he had never seen before. He looked around, trying to get his bearings.

A different officer entered the room, closing the door behind him.

Eno stood. "As a guest on your planet, I admit I expected a better greeting than this."

"Cut the bull. Where are you from?"

"I'm from Chroma, a planet in the Vaedra System."

"You look like a military man, what's your name, rank and serial number?"

"I'm Eno ni Esrith, pilot, first class, on the Concordance, a Class A Star Destroyer. I piloted Shadow One here to deliver Councilors Contor and Thebes from the Vaedra System, along with Adam Davis of Earth."

"We found no ID on you. Where's your ID?"

"I don't know what that is."

"Come on! It's your identification. Where is it?"

Eno pointed to the insignia on his jumper. "I'm a pilot of the Concordance. Here is my proof."

"That's not an ID. I'm afraid you'll have to stay here until I see it."

"I'm wearing the unicrin of an officer/pilot of the Concordance. What further proof do you need?"

"An ID! I want your damn ID. Everyone has an ID."

"Maybe on Earth, but where I come from, this insignia is proof of who I am."

The officer turned and left the room.

Contor paced back and forth in his small quarters when an officer entered. "Good evening," Contor offered.

"How do you know it's evening?"

"It was morning when I arrived in your atmosphere, so I assumed it is much later than that now."

"Yes. Where we captured you, it is, but where you are now, it's much earlier in the day."

Contor's puzzled look made the officer grin.

"Who are you and where do you come from?"

Contor strained to read the officer's name on his badge.

"Well, Officer Getz, I'm from the planet Tarsius, where I was elected by my peers to represent them on the Council of Nations. My name is Contor de Llave. I am a history professor at the Academy on Tarsius."

"Llave? Isn't that Spanish for key?"

"Maybe on your planet, but on Tarsius, it is our language and my father's name. I was sent here, along with Councilor Thebes from Vestra Major, to represent the entire Vaedra System in sharing technology with Earth."

"Uh, huh. And do you have any ID?"

"ID, what is that?"

"Your identification. Doesn't anyone on your planet carry identification on them?"

"No. People take our word for who we are. Do your people carry identification?"

"Yes."

"Why is that?"

"There are too many people on planet Earth. And some people lie about their identity."

"How long do you plan on keeping us separated?"

"As long as it takes." Getz turned and left the room.

Thebes sat on his bunk, legs crossed and arms resting on his knees. He was meditating on calming thoughts when the officer burst into the room. His eyes opened, spying a large man leering at him with arms crossed over a barrel chest.

"Can I help you, officer?"

"I don't suppose you have any ID?"

"Idea about what?"

"I didn't say 'idea', I said 'ID'. Identification."

"I am Thebes of Telman from the planet Vestra Major. I am a professor of Economics at the Academy on Vestra Major. I was elected to the Council of Nations—"

"Cut the crap! I want your ID and I want it now!"

"You can *want* it, sir, but you can't *have* what doesn't exist."

The officer stormed out of the room.

Adam awoke from a groggy sleep, his head pounding. "**Genesis, can you hear me?**" He rubbed his temples.

"**I can hear you, Adam. Are you all right?**"

"**Yes, I've been separated from the others. I'm not even sure if we're still at NASA. Did you go to plan B?**"

"**Yes, hours ago we spoke to the President. We're awaiting security clearances. Jeremy gave us his phone**" before they returned him home if you need to call us. Adam, I love you."

"I love you, too, Gen."

He thought about what she said. Hours ago they spoke to the President. How long did they wait before leaving the Concordance? With the time it would take to fly to the White House, it must be late afternoon or early evening. And how long did it take them to get to *see* the President once they got there?

He heard the knob on the door jiggle so he turned to face it. The door slammed open. The loud bang startled him.

A big, burly military man stood before him, taking up the expanse of the door frame, his hands on his hips.

24

FALSE LEADERS

*A*dam jumped from his bed, his hands fisted. A small, gray figure stepped from behind Officer Getz.

"Who were you speaking to?" a strange voice said in Adam's head. Adam glared at the gray alien. **"None of your damn business!"**

"So, you are telepathic?"

"Where's your ID?" Getz barked out the question.

"It's at home."

"And where is that? Some planet in the Vaedra system?"

"No. I'm from Tennessee. I left it at home. I was abducted and didn't have it on me at the time."

"You expect me to believe that crap?"

"Look, I don't care what you believe. I was abducted from my home in Tennessee. I was taken to the Vaedra System where I...never mind. It's a long story. I got the Vaedran Council of Nations to come back with me to share technology with Earth but some general stole our ship and hijacked us from Kennedy Space Center. I don't know where we are, but you better get us back to Washington, D.C., or there will be hell to pay."

"Washington?"

"Yes. The President knows we're here and he'll be looking for us."

"You're not going anywhere. Who do you think you are, telling *me* what to do?" Getz walked up to Adam, forcing him to back into the wall. "I tell *you* what to do, you little punk."

"Leave him. He's been communicating with someone from outside."

Getz' eyes grew large and he swung around. "How do you know this?"

"He was speaking to someone when we entered the room."

Getz turned back to Adam. "Are you a telepath?"

"I wouldn't tell you if I was."

Getz turned to leave then swung around and back-handed Adam across the face, knocking him back against the wall.

"Now I see who's in charge here, and it sure as hell isn't the U.S. Army!" Adam shouted as the two left the room.

"Genesis, can you hear me?"

"Yes, Adam."

"The grays are calling the shots around here. They're telepathic. Be careful."

25

WASHINGTON, D.C

CABINET ROOM, WHITE HOUSE

"*I*'m sorry this is such short notice, but a series of events have occurred that require immediate attention and possible national security," the President addressed his Cabinet members.

Keely McGuire sat on a long bench beside Genesis and Tremol, with Tom Gowan standing beside her. They were a few feet behind some seats at the table. The gathered group of men and women began whispering among themselves.

"I'll get right to it," the President began. "We have some special guests here in this room from the Vaedra System which is in another part of our galaxy. They have come to share technology with us, but someone at NASA has taken it upon themselves to appropriate their spaceship and relocate our guests, along with a fellow citizen of the United States."

"I'll take care of NASA," the Secretary of Defense said.

"It's not only NASA that concerns me," the President said. He glanced over at Genesis. "Show them what you showed me."

Genesis stepped toward the general with the scanner box, setting it on the table before him. She hit the replay button on the vid-screen. The general watched as their ship, the Concordance, was shot at by a spaceship with 'USA' emblazoned on it. "What the hell?" he said.

"Keep watching," the President urged.

The vid-screen showed images of the moon's village and compounds on the dark side. The general glanced at him. "Is this our moon?"

"Yes. Someone has been lying to us and the American people for far too long." He glanced around the room. "Did any of you know about this before today?" Everyone shook their heads.

"This is a catastrophe. Not only do we have a secret space military actively shooting at passing spaceships, but a base on the moon."

The Secretary of Homeland Security spoke up. "Sir, this is not only a case of national security, but Homeland Security as well. How can we effectively protect our citizens from space aliens when we have all these problems at our borders?"

"Exactly," he said.

"How did the military prepare a space command group under our noses without telling anyone? And how did they fund it?" the general chimed in.

Another Secretary added, "We need to have an investigation into this matter. This is unacceptable!"

"You're right, but we don't have time for that now. We have four people missing from a landing party that we've got to find."

Tremol stood up. "Sorry to interrupt, sir, but I just got word from Admiral Esrith of the Concordance. He says that if we don't return the landing party safely within twenty-four hours, he will annihilate this planet and everyone on it."

"Can he do that?" someone said.

"Yes, he can. The Concordance is a Class A Star Destroyer. Admiral Esrith has turned many airless planets into asteroids in other galaxies. One of those men in the landing party is his son, Eno. If anything happens to him, he won't hesitate to destroy your world," Tremol said.

Gowan nudged Keely's shoulder with his elbow. She stood.

"Sir, with the assistance of the general, I'm sure I can help these people find their landing party," she said. *God help me!*

The President looked at his Cabinet. "We have some tough decisions to make tonight and I hope we can get Congress on board or we don't stand a chance."

Genesis touched her head and glanced at Tremol.

"What is it?" Tremol asked.

"The grays are in control of your military," she said to the President.

"The U.S. Military?" The President asked.

Genesis nodded. "I just heard from Adam."

"How are they controlling our military?" the President asked the Secretary of Defense.

The general stood and glanced at Keely. "I just got word that your clearances have gone through. You've got my number." He turned back to the President. "I will personally find out, sir." The general followed Keely and the others out of the room and handed Genesis her scanner.

"You text me when you get clear and on every step of the way. I'll find out what's going on," the general said to her. The two exchanged phone numbers.

Keely turned to Tremol and Genesis. "We're good to go." She ushered the two of them out of the office, while the general made phone calls in the hall.

She headed to her supervisor's office where she collected a power cord for the phone and a box of ammo.

"What is that?" Tremol asked.

"Ammunition," she said.

"And what does it do?"

"It's for killing people who try to kill us," she said, hoping she wouldn't have to use it.

"We have better weapons," he said.

"Of course you do." *Smart ass.* "Now, show me your spaceship."

The three of them left the White House through the front door.

Genesis powered up the ship from the scanner box, briefly hitting the de-cloaking button.

"Oh, now that's cool," Keely said. She looked over the triangular-shaped object before going up the ramp. She had mixed emotions about this whole thing. First her parents were abducted and now this. What if they *had* been taken by the grays? All the online research she had done left more questions than answers.

Genesis quickly cloaked the ship again.

"Here are our weapons," Tremol showed her the storage area with what looked like rifles and smaller weapons. "These will work on half stun and full stun." He handed her the smaller weapon. Tremol was incredibly close. She felt her heart rate kick up again.

He showed her how to use the weapon, and caught her gaze. "You don't have to kill anyone. Half stun will paralyze the target for a few minutes, so you can restrain them. Full stun will knock them out for a couple hours." She handed the weapon back to him.

"Yes, and their heads will hurt and their bodies feel weak when coming out of stun," Genesis added.

"And these laser rifles will kill," Tremol added. "We only use these if we are forced to."

"Ah, but I only have this one." She pulled her Sig from

her holster. Tremol reached his hand out to her, demanding the surrender of her gun.

"You're not taking my Sig," she said, glaring at him.

"It will be safe here," he said. "Besides, it could damage the ship if you miss your target." His gaze was unwavering.

"I never miss." She glared back at him, still holding her weapon.

"He will win the staring contest. I suggest you turn over your weapon and use one of ours," Genesis said.

"Fine!" She reluctantly handed over her weapon. It felt like giving up a piece of her soul. She watched him carefully stow it in a compartment, along with her box of ammo.

"So where's my new weapon?" she asked, her hands on her hips.

"You'll get one when needed. Now strap in," Tremol ordered.

He pointed to the back seats, where she reluctantly sat and strapped herself in. This was not how she pictured this going down. She felt naked without her Sig in its holster. She glanced at her watch. Twenty-three hours, twenty-eight minutes and counting.

26

WHITE HOUSE
WASHINGTON, D.C.

*T*remol went through the pre-flight steps while Keely fastened her safety harness. She seemed optimistic about finding the landing party, so he would try to be more optimistic himself. He just couldn't get over a nagging feeling in his gut that something was a little off about the whole situation.

Genesis sat beside him. "Anything left for me to do?"

"No, I'm done with pre-flight. Where to?"

Genesis looked over her shoulder at Keely. "We need your coordinates to get started."

"My coordinates? I guess we skipped that part." She searched her phone for the general's number and texted him. "We could try Area 51," she said.

"What is that?" he asked.

"It's a place the government denies but everyone knows it exists. Do you have a map of sorts on this ship?"

Genesis typed in "map" while Tremol lifted Shadow Two off the ground.

"Are we still cloaked?" Keely asked.

"Yes," he responded, pulling the ship higher into the atmosphere.

"Will they be able to see us on radar?"

"I'm not sure what you mean by radar," he began, "but we cannot be detected by sensors. We can, however, detect other ships around us, whether they are cloaked or not."

"How can you do that?"

"You'll have to ask the scientists those questions."

Keely glanced at her phone. "I've got your coordinates." She unhooked her safety straps and moved between Genesis and him, showing them the phone.

"Got it," Genesis said as she punched in the coordinates.

"You'd better buckle in or you'll be riding the back wall," he said, winking at her. Did he just see her eyes grow wide?

Keely strapped herself back in the seat. "All set here," she said.

A quick glance allowed him to see Keely had turned a bright pink color. "You've changed colors, just like Adam does."

Genesis glanced back to see it, too. "Do all Earthens change colors?" she asked.

Keely covered her face with her hands. "You're embarrassing me! Stop it! Stop it, now."

Genesis smiled. Tremol felt himself smile as well.

This Keely was pleasant to look at, even with all those tiny spots of brown on her face and that orange hair. She did resemble the Huanti people, right down to her bright blue eyes.

Keely pulled out her phone and punched in a number. "If I don't call my mother, she'll worry about me," she said.

He glanced back at her. "That's her job," he said.

"Hey Mom. I just wanted to let you know I'll be out of town a few days. I've got an assignment that will keep me busy."

"I didn't recognize the number," her mother said.

"This is my work number. I left my phone at home so don't call me unless it's an emergency, okay?"

"Sure, honey. Be careful."

"I will. Have you gotten your results from the MRIs yet?"

"No, but I'll let you know as soon as I do."

"Love you, Mom, bye."

He smiled as he heard her conversation. He hadn't talked to his mother in quite a while. He would have to make a point of doing that when he got back to Vestra Major. But the thought of contacting his mother reminded him of Admiral Esrith's son, Eno. "I told Esrith that Adam had seen visions of the grays before they left in Shadow One. We need to let him know we're definitely dealing with them."

Genesis opened the comm-link.

"Admiral, this is Lieutenant Tremol."

"Go ahead. Any news?"

"Yes. It seems the grays *are* controlling the military here on Earth."

"Now you'll see why I wanted to be a part of this mission," Esrith said.

"Sir?"

"This is why the I.S.P. bet against you. Only they didn't know the extent of my training."

"I don't understand."

"I came prepared, Tremol."

He glanced at Genesis. She shook her head and shrugged.

"Thank you, sir. We're heading to where the group may be located. We'll let you know when we get there."

"I have a lock on your position. I'll be able to track you."

"Can you locate Shadow One?" he asked.

"No. They did something to the scanner, so I can't track them."

He made sure they were high enough in the atmosphere to still see the land mass. As they got closer to their coordinates, he realized the sky was lighter.

"We are approaching the coordinates now," Genesis said.

He lowered the ship for the approach.

Keely unfastened her straps again. "That was quick. We haven't been in the air that long, have we?" she asked, kneeling between him and Genesis once more.

He hid a smile and noticed a faint smell of flowers. He found himself leaning toward her.

"Is that your hair that smells like flowers?"

"It's my shampoo. Don't you have shampoo with fragrances?"

"What is shampoo?" he asked, glancing her way.

Their gazes met and he forgot that he had been banking the ship.

"Watch out!" Genesis shouted, punching him in the arm. He caught himself and pulled up before hitting a rock formation.

"That was close, Tremol," Genesis said. She scowled at him.

Keely fell against his seat. "I guess I'd better strap in again."

"Where should we land?" he asked.

The place was lit up like Vaedra. Below them was a massive field, in the middle of nowhere, surround by mountains. On the field were hangers built into the mountains. Several doors opened and spaceships flew out onto the field. He set their ship down at the far end where there were no hangars.

The three of them watched as five ships pulled straight up and flew in an arrow formation heading east, where they had come from.

"What are they doing with spaceships out here?" Keely asked.

"Where do you get your ships from?" Genesis asked her.

"The U.S. government doesn't own spaceships," Keely said.

"Didn't you see the vid-screen we showed your President?" he asked.

"No."

Genesis punched in the information on the scanner and showed Keely what she had shown the general.

"Oh my gosh! Now I wish I had taken pictures of those ships. I could send it to the general."

Tremol used the Nav-U-Com and pulled up the footage of the spaceships. "Will this help?"

"Oh, yes!" Keely squeezed his neck, then took pictures of the footage with her phone. She texted the general the images.

"Now we need to see if your landing party is here." Keely stood and pulled his arm. "I'll take that weapon now, if you don't mind."

He rose from his seat and retrieved weapons for all of them, her slight squeeze of his neck still fresh on his mind. He handed out holsters as well.

"I think I'll use my own holster with this weapon," she said.

"It won't fit." He shook his head and proceeded to put on his holster.

Genesis strapped her holster on her thigh. Keely watched her. She tried to put hers on like Genesis did.

"You're doing it wrong." He moved close to her and tried to show her how to put it on. Keely pushed his chest. "We don't stand this close to people."

He grabbed her hands. "I'm trying to teach you how to put on the holster. Stop fighting me."

"You're in my personal space and it makes me uncomfortable." She locked gazes with him. He would not back down on this matter. She had to learn how to use their equipment. She finally pulled her hands free.

"This is for when you don't need to kill anyone, just knock them out." He showed her how to use the weapon again and handed it to her.

Reluctantly, Keely took it and put it in her new thigh holster. She still wore her thick vest she had on earlier.

Genesis used the scanner to open the ramp.

"Hey, do you have a cloaking device for people?" Keely asked.

"That's an excellent question, Keely, but no." He ushered her down before him. Genesis had already started down the ramp, her weapon ready. Keely held her weapon with both hands, glancing around. He felt exposed in this vast field. "Let's get to cover," he said.

Genesis closed the ramp and joined him and Keely at a half-opened hangar. Keely flopped down on the ground and looked under the hangar door. "All clear," she whispered. She scurried under the doorway. He and Genesis followed her.

"There's nothing here. Let's check out that door over there," Keely said.

The three of them made a run for the door. He peeked between the door and frame then motioned for everyone to follow. They ran down a long hallway until they came to another door.

Keely looked inside first. He stood behind her and saw Shadow One. She motioned for them to follow. He moved close to her without touching her. Why was she like that? Her skin begged to be touched. And her orange hair began to come loose in places.

"That's Shadow One," he whispered in her ear.

They slipped inside the hangar, where the outer door was closed. He searched the left side, Keely went right. Genesis punched some buttons on the scanner and the Shadow One came to life.

No one was in the hangar but the three of them. "Genesis, try speaking to Adam. See if he is here," he said.

Genesis closed her eyes.

"Can you fly this thing out of here?" Keely whispered to him. She stood on tiptoes to reach his ear.

Her breath sent tingles up his spine. He glanced at her. How did she do that? Now she was unbearably close to him and it didn't seem to bother her. "If Genesis can get Shadow One to accept the codes from Shadow Two, then yes, I can fly this out of here."

"We'll have to find a way to open the hangar," Keely said. She glanced around, looking for a button to open the door, and caught sight of Genesis' necklace glowing.

Genesis turned her necklace over and then looked up at him and Keely.

"Adam is not here, but I've got his coordinates. He said the grays think he is a telepath."

"I didn't know he was," Tremol said.

"He isn't, unless his skill has grown. He was only able to speak with me."

"Ok, so we need to get this ship out of here. Can you and Tremol make that happen?" Keely asked.

"I can try," Genesis said as she pressed some buttons on the scanner.

"I'll see if I can find a way to open the hangar door," Keely said.

"I hear voices," Tremol said.

Genesis pressed another button and opened the ramp. "Get inside, quick!"

27

CONCORDANCE

*A*dmiral Esrith sat at his command chair.

"Captain Melbus, we're dealing with the grays. Get out the frequency modulator. We're going to find out where those gray bastards are hiding."

"Aye, Admiral!"

Captain Melbus hurried below decks to arouse the crew.

"All hands on deck!" he called. "This is not a drill!"

CABINET ROOM, WHITE HOUSE
WASHINGTON, D.C.

"Ladies and gentlemen, we've got to tell the American people about this," the President said to his Cabinet members.

"There will be chaos and panic," one of the Secretaries said.

"I think there would be more chaos if they found out they were betrayed by their own government," said another.

"I think you're right," the President said. "The best way to deal with this is honesty. Get me the press secretary."

AREA 51

*T*remol, Keely and Genesis crammed inside Shadow One and headed for the Nav-U-Com. Keely squatted between him and Genesis and watched out the viewport.

"Can they hear us?" Keely whispered.

"No, but we can hear them." He turned a few knobs and pressed some buttons on the Nav-U-Com.

"I can't wait to get this baby in the air," one Air Force pilot said to the other.

"Once we figure out how to use this thing, we'll be set," the other one said while holding up the Shadow One scanner.

"He's got our scanner!" Genesis said. She quickly locked the ramp.

"Can they get inside?" Keely asked.

"Maybe," Tremol responded. He glanced at Keely. "We need to hide." He stood.

Genesis and Keely stood, following him. He opened a storage unit near the ramp and pushed Genesis inside, along with the scanner. Then on the other side of the Nav-

U-Com, he opened another storage unit and climbed inside, pulling Keely inside with him.

He held his breath. The space was very tight as she pressed against his body. She faced him, her head against his chest. She was slightly taller than Genesis, but he'd never been this close to Genesis. Keely's firm arms and legs felt muscular and solid, but her skin was soft. And what was that bulky thing she wore around her middle? It must be some type of body armor for protection.

He heard a sound coming from across the ship. The ramp lowered. Then the voices sounded again. "So far, so good," one pilot said.

He heard the ramp close. "This is the fun part," the other one responded.

As the pilot talked, Tremol's body tensed, trying to get Keely's attention. If only she could open the door? He couldn't move his arm in the tight space. She looked up at his face, and he nodded. She tried to reach back behind her for the latch on the door but couldn't find it. He reached for it, pressing her into the door and into his side. His hand brushed her butt and he felt her tense at his touch. He found the handle, releasing the latch. The door sprang open and Keely hopped out and spun around. He had his stun weapon out and fired twice. Both men slumped over.

He heard Genesis banging on her door. "Let her out," he ordered. He pulled one of the pilots out of his seat and set him in the back.

Keely opened the storage door. "The latch was stuck," Genesis said.

Genesis and Keely removed the other man. "What should we do with him?" Genesis asked.

"I say toss them out into the hangar and take off," Keely suggested.

"No. Restrain them. We'll need them both for questioning," Tremol said. He sat in the pilot's seat.

Keely glanced at Genesis. "I don't have any handcuffs."

Genesis pulled four plastic strips off her holster. "I have yetik!" She handed two to Keely.

Keely watched Genesis use the first restraint, then did the same for her pilot.

"Strap in!" Tremol ordered. It would be a matter of time before someone missed the two pilots. He quickly finished pre-flight while the two women finished restraining the two men.

Keely sat in her seat and put on her harness. Both men were on the floor beneath her. Genesis strapped in as well.

Before he heard Keely's safety harness click, he had them in the air. "We are cloaked. I will drop you off at Shadow Two and hover until you're in the air. From there, we'll head to the coordinates you got from Adam."

Genesis put the coordinates she got on her communicator into Shadow One's database.

He landed next to Shadow Two, blocking the opening of that ship with his own ship. Keely moved into Genesis' seat.

Before Genesis had closed her ramp on Shadow Two, a voice came over the pilot's radio.

"Come in, Major, this is Flight Control."

He and Keely looked at each other. "Don't answer it!" she said.

He pulled up to give Genesis room to take off. He had her on his vid-screen in cloaked mode.

"Major, this is Flight Control, do you read?"

Genesis pulled up and headed west. He followed.

"Major, come in! This is Flight Control."

Keely pulled out her phone and texted the general.

Tremol opened the comm-link. "Admiral Esrith, come in, this is Tremol."

"Go ahead, Tremol, what have you got?"

A GRAY AREA

"*A*dmiral, we have Shadow One and we are headed to the coordinates Adam has given us. Can you lock onto our position?"

"Locking on...now! We got you both. Good work, Tremol. We are using the frequency modulator and are locating the holes the grays have carved out on Earth. We'll let you know when we've completed the work. You have less than nineteen hours to complete your mission."

"Yes, sir." He clicked off the comm-link.

"Nineteen hours before doomsday," Keely said.

"What is doomsday?"

"The end of the Earth." Keely sobered at the thought of not seeing her parents anymore. "You know, I just found out that my parents were...abducted. At least, they think they were. A UFO followed them home one night. They don't remember anything after getting home, but woke up the next day in bed."

"You think it was the grays?"

"I don't know what to think. That's their M.O. I mean, here you are, an alien sitting next to me. You don't look like an alien or sound like one and we're having a conversation. I am sitting in a spaceship, having a conversation with an alien." Keely shook her head. The thought was bizarre.

Tremol smiled. "Aliens come in all shapes and sizes. You'd be surprised how many planets out there have humans on them."

"Have you been to a lot of planets?"

"All the planets in the Vaedra System, of course. All of them are humans, they're just different races. When I was training for the I.S.P., I went out to the Pleiades."

"Is that far from Earth?"

"It's actually closer than Vaedra."

This man was not only good looking but interesting. And when he smiled, her heart lightened as well.

"I almost forgot! I didn't tell the general that we're dealing with the grays," she said. She pulled out her phone and called the Secretary of Defense. She filled him in on what Admiral Esrith was doing with frequency modulators. When she finished, she realized they were coming up on the Pacific coast.

She scratched her head and realized her hair was coming out of the tight bun she had fixed earlier this morning. "My hair must be a mess," she said. She tried to smooth it into place.

"That's an interesting ring," Tremol said, catching her hand. His touch was gentle, but his hand felt strong.

"Oh, thanks. I got it from my boyfriend," she said, pulling it off to show him. "It's a poison ring." She opened it to show him the inside. "This is where someone would put the poison."

"Why would they do that?"

"To kill themselves or someone else."

"Have you used it like that?"

"No, I just like the colors. It's an antique ring."

He gazed into her eyes. "What is a boyfriend?"

"He's a guy that I'm seeing."

"Are you mates?"

"Mates? What do you mean?" *Was he talking about her sex life?*

"On Vaedra, men take mates for life, usually by the age of twenty for men and eighteen for women."

"Do you have a mate?"

"Unfortunately, no. I've spent all my time training to be the best I.S.P. agent I could, I didn't have time to meet anyone. Now, it's too late."

"It's not too late. People get married at all ages here."

"So, this boyfriend is not your mate?"

"Well, if he asks me to marry him, then I would consider being his mate."

"You love him, then?"

"Well, yeah. I guess I do."

He studied her face. "You aren't sure, are you?"

"Well, maybe not. I don't know him as well as I'd like to. But I spent all my time training as well. I met him at a party when I first got assigned to Washington. He was the first man to give me any attention."

Keely pulled the elastic band out of her hair and shook her head to loosen her curls. Then she ran her fingers through it to comb it out.

Tremol looked up and saw Genesis in Shadow Two dive into the ocean. He followed her, locking on her position.

"We're going under water?" Keely asked, bracing herself for the dive.

"Yes."

"Won't this thing leak?"

Tremol glanced at her and smiled. "It's airtight. It can withstand space!"

Keely looked through the viewport and could see only darkness and an occasional fish. Around Shadow Two, there was a glow that enabled them to see more of their surroundings.

"Do we have that glow around us as well?"

"Yes, we do."

He reached out and touched her hair, massaging her scalp as well, sending a strange feeling throughout her body. "It feels soft," he said, slowly pulling his hand away.

"Thanks. How did you *think* it would feel?" She missed his touch already.

"Rough, hard."

Keely heard the two men stirring behind them. "I'll shoot them again," She unfastened her safety belt.

Tremol grabbed her arm. "No, it's time for questions."

Keely faced the two pilots. "Who are you working for?" she asked.

"We're U.S. Air Force pilots," one of them answered.

"Really? Since when does the Air Force steal spaceships?"

"We didn't steal that ship," the other answered.

"How did it get to Area 51?"

"Area 51 doesn't exist," the first one answered.

"Bullshit! How do you think we found you?"

"We work for the U.S. Air Force!"

"And I work for Secret Service! Answer the damn question!" Keely pulled her stun weapon on the two men and pointed it at their faces.

"CIA! CIA!" the second pilot answered.

"You work for the CIA?"

"We work for the U.S. Air Force. The CIA controls Area 51. We were sent here as test pilots. CIA calls the shots."

"Did you know the grays are controlling the military here?"

"The grays?" the first pilot asked.

"Yes, the grays. Four people were abducted by our government and taken here with this ship. Where are they?"

The pilot's eyes grew large as he looked beyond Keely's shoulder.

"There! They were taken there," he nodded.

Keely looked behind her and saw a massive compound under the ocean, lit up like a stadium at night. She holstered her weapon.

"What the hell is that?" She straightened, grabbing Tremol's seat for balance.

"Left! Go left!" the pilot shouted. Tremol did as he was told. Keely lost her balance and fell against Tremol's seat. He wrapped his arm around her waist and pulled her against the arm rest.

"Stay!" he shouted.

"Through that opening," the pilot added.

Tremol went through the opening and found a docking station. It opened, and his ship was taken up into the docking bay.

Tremol grabbed her arm firmly and faced her. "It's imperative that you keep your safety harness on at all times. You could have been hurt and I could have crashed this ship."

"Got it. Sorry." Keely tried to free herself from his grip, but he didn't let go. He stood and pulled her up in front of him.

"Are you all right?"

She nodded. He finally released her, and she straightened herself up. That was close.

The two pilots had been tossed around as well and Tremol and Keely helped them up.

"I need to let the general know where we are," she said, pulling out her phone. She dialed his number. Something weird happened and her call didn't go through. She tried texting him but the message wasn't delivered.

"Let me try," Tremol said. He hit the comm-link to reach Admiral Esrith.

"Come in, Concordance, this is Lieutenant Tremol," he said into the comms.

No answer. He looked at Keely and shrugged. He tried again with no answer.

"Come in Shadow Two, this is Shadow One."

No answer.

"Maybe the signal is being blocked," Keely suggested.

"It is. They won't let anything go out unless approved by General Yermolay," one of the pilots said.

"Have you been here before?" Keely asked.

"Yes. We fly the ships down here to run through tests."

Once the water cleared, they could see that Genesis had parked in front of them.

When Tremol opened the ramp, a large group of military men hustled out to greet them, weapons in hand.

"Great! A party." Keely said.

31

SPACE FORCE COMMAND

ajor Sinclair stood before Major Getz at Area 51.

"Where the hell are the extraterrestrial visitors, sir?"

"We have no visitors here. Get the hell out of my office," he barked.

Sinclair leaned over Getz's desk. "Because of you, we have a major incident facing our government. These people were not acting alone. There is a large battleship above our atmosphere. The communications we got is they are looking for their people. Unless you return these people to me, NOW, I will hand your ass to you on a platter. You got that, sir?"

Getz jumped up from his seat and went to the door. He held it open for Sinclair, without a word.

Sinclair left the office. Once outside the complex, he called Forshen.

"Major Forshen here."

"Sir, Yermolay's people are playing hardball. I got nothing from Major Getz."

"Then we'll take them down one at a time, starting with Chief Dallin at NASA."

"Yes, sir."

32

UNDERWATER BASE

PACIFIC OCEAN

General Yermolay sat in his office, waiting for the visitors to be brought to him. A knock on the door alerted him that they were present.

"Come in," he said aloud. A couple of guards escorted Genesis, Tremol, Keely, and the two pilots into the office.

"Well, welcome to our undersea base. Have a seat," Yermolay said.

There were no seats in his office, so everyone stood.

"What are you two doing here?" Yermolay asked the two pilots.

"We were captured by these people when we tried to fly the ship that was brought to Dreamland."

"Oh? And who the hell are these people?"

"I am Tremol and this is Genesis. We are both from the Vaedra System. We have come to pick up our landing party that you abducted and return them to our home."

Keely stepped forward. "I'm Keely McGuire, a Secret Service agent, working on behalf of the President and I'm here to escort these people and the people you illegally captured back to the White House as guests of the President."

"You don't say? Well, I don't know what you are talking about. We have no one here from the Vaedra System—"

"You lie!" Genesis shouted. "Adam is here. I've tracked him to this place. I have spoken to him."

"You're mistaken." Yermolay pushed a button on his desk.

"I wouldn't do that if I were you." Tremol stepped forward.

"Are you threatening me, boy?"

"Yes, I am."

A couple of officers and uniformed soldiers stepped into the office.

"Admiral Esrith is in control of the Concordance, a Class A Star Destroyer. If you don't return our people to us immediately, he will destroy this planet and everyone on it."

"Well, I have something that can destroy his ship."

"If you are working with the grays, I assure you, you do not. We have fought the grays and kept them out of our system for more than two decades. Admiral Esrith is locating all the hiding places you call bases that the grays had you build. With one button, he can destroy all of those bases. Is that what you want? Do you want to be the one who causes the..." He looked at Keely. "The doomsday of Earth?"

"General, you must understand, you cannot take the ships that belong to visitors from another system. Come with us to Washington and tell the President what is going on here," Keely pleaded.

"Take these prisoners to their new accommodations," General Yermolay ordered his people.

"The President and the Secretary of Defense know where we are. You answer to them if anything happens to us," Keely said. She pulled away from the guard who tried to hold her.

"I answer to no one," Yermolay said. "And they will never find you. They don't even know this base exists."

"We found you!" Keely shouted.

"Admiral Esrith has our coordinates to this place and has a lock on our position," Tremol added.

"And I sent the coordinates to the Secretary of Defense, just before we got here."

The general pointed toward the door. "I gave you orders!" he shouted.

The soldiers physically removed them from the office.

33

CONCORDANCE

*A*dmiral Esrith drummed his fingers on his chin. The information he got from Tremol led him to believe they were at the base where the landing party was being held.

"Did you get a fix on Genesis' medallion, Captain Melbus?"

"Yes sir."

"Pull it up on the vid-screen."

The vid-screen showed all the tunnels the grays had built. Then a double pulsing sounded, superimposed on the tunnels map, but it wasn't in a gray tunnel.

"Interesting. It looks like two separate pulses. They may be safe where they are. Have they responded to any hails?"

"No sir."

"Sir, we're getting a hail from another source," the communications officer said.

"Go ahead," Esrith said.

The communications officer opened the frequency.

"Hello, this is Space Force Command, can you read?"

"Yes, we read you. Go ahead."

"Identify yourself, please."

"I am Admiral Esrith of the Concordance, a Class A Star Destroyer. We are here on a diplomatic mission to share technology and open trade relations with your planet. Four of our people were captured when they landed. Another crew is in search of them now and are not answering our hails."

"We apologize for the misunderstanding, Admiral, and we will assist you in finding your party. Are you planning on landing?"

"No, we have a fix on all the gray tunnels and we will destroy them if our people are not returned in the next ten hours, Earth time."

"Admiral, we can't possibly find them that quickly."

"We have a fix on them right now, if you'd like the coordinates."

"Yes, sir."

"Comm Officer, please send the coordinates of our party."

"Yes, sir."

"Oh, and open communications with them one more time."

"Yes, sir. Go ahead."

"Space Force Command, this is the Concordance, can you read?"

"Yes, Admiral, go ahead."

"You may want to contact your President as he is also waiting to hear from our people. One of his agents is escorting our second team."

"The U.S. President, sir?"

"Yes. Don't you communicate with your leader?"

"Uh, yes sir."

34

UNDERWATER BASE
PACIFIC OCEAN

*M*ore guards joined the group as Tremol, Keely and Genesis were led down a long corridor. Tremol still wore his communicator, which the guards mistook as a watch in their search. And Genesis still wore her medallion. He hoped she had located Adam while they were walking. He turned his head to see if Keely was all right. Just behind her the two pilots were shoved into a room together. The guard slammed the door.

The guard in front of them opened a door and shoved him inside. As he regained his balance, Keely and Genesis joined him.

"Admiral Esrith, come in, this is Tremol," he spoke into his communicator.

"Tremol, go ahead. Esrith here. Have you found Eno?"

"We are in an underwater structure of some kind. Genesis located Adam's signal. We are trying to find him and then search for the others."

"We've heard from the Space Force Command. They said they would help us find you but we have Genesis' signal on the vid-screen, as well as Adam's. He is a few feet to your right."

He looked at Genesis. "Talk to him."

Genesis called to Adam with her mind. While she spoke to Adam, he moved to the door, but Keely was already picking the lock with some metallic object.

"Come on you two, let's go!" she whispered.

He patted her on the back, impressed with her initiative.

Looking out into the empty hall, Keely motioned for them to follow. He moved behind her, with Genesis behind him. "In here," Genesis whispered loudly. She pointed to the next door in the hall.

Keely headed back and worked on the lock. The door swung open.

"Gen!" Adam called out.

"Shhhh!" Keely warned. "Let's go!"

Adam scooped Genesis up in his arms and kissed her. They headed to the next room and Keely picked the lock, while the others watched the hall.

"I hear footsteps," Genesis said.

Keely tried one more time and got the door opened and they all pushed into the room, keeping the door ajar. Inside was Councilor Thebes.

"Oh, thank the heavens! Is everyone all right?" Thebes asked.

"We're still looking for Eno and Contor," Tremol said. "Any idea where they might be?"

"No."

Keely listened at the door. "I don't hear anything." She pulled the door open. Tremol stood over her and looked out into the hall.

"This time, only Keely and I will search the next room. The rest of you stay here until we signal to you. Genesis, keep watch at the door."

Keely tried her hand once more and finally unlocked the next door. He pushed it open to see Contor, alone, inside.

He signaled for Genesis to bring everyone and they gathered in Contor's room.

"We've got to find Eno. Admiral Esrith is set to destroy the grays' tunnels," he said.

"Tunnels?" Adam asked.

"Yes, they are all over your Earth but mostly in your continent."

"How did he find them?"

"With a frequency modulator."

"How many are there?" Contor asked.

"He didn't say but I'm sure it's too many," Tremol said.

"I suggest we get moving if we are to find Eno. We're running out of time and I want to stay alive if at all possible," Keely added.

"What is she talking about?" Contor asked.

"Yes, and who is she?" Adam asked.

"This is Keely McGuire, a Secret Service agent, working with your President to help us find you. However, Admiral Esrith gave us only twenty-four hours to find and return you all or he would destroy your Earth," Tremol said.

"What?"

"Yes, and we're down to less than ten hours if my calculations are correct," Keely said.

"The rest of you remain here while Keely and I attempt to gain entrance on the next room. We'll signal for you when ready," he said.

Tremol ushered Keely through the doorway and they tried the last door. It took longer to get this one unlocked. When Tremol pushed the door open, Eno sat on the edge of his bunk, gagged, with hands and feet tied and General Yermolay leaning against the small sink.

"We've been expecting you. Come in, come in."

35

WHITE HOUSE,
WASHINGTON, D.C.

*T*he President paced back and forth in his Oval Office while his Secretary of Defense updated him on the whereabouts of Keely McGuire and the visitors.

"I've discovered the Black Projects funded the Space Force since the 1960s, as well as other covert operations resulting in technological advances which weren't all shared with Defense. Agent McGuire and her party were captured in an underwater base, where we tracked her with the phone I gave her, but we haven't gotten a response. I believe they must be captured by our own people in the Black Government. The nearest sub won't be able to reach them in time."

"I can't believe they kept everyone in the dark this long. We need to go to the American people and let them know. I've got the Press Secretary working on something now."

A knock sounded on the door before it opened.

"Sir, I think you need to see this," a Secret Service agent said. He ushered the President into a room with a television set to a cable news network.

"This just in: a prominent Washington newspaper is reporting the landing of a UFO at the White House. The visitors from the Vaedra System are looking for their missing landing party and threatened to destroy the Earth if the landing party isn't returned within twenty-four hours."

"How did this get out?" The President looked to his Secretary of Defense.

"I have no idea, sir, but I'll look into it."

The phone in the room rang.

"Get my secretary," he said as the General left the room.

36

UNDERWATER BASE
PACIFIC OCEAN

*K*eely looked at Eno, then at Yermolay.

"What are you doing?" she said, moving toward Eno.

Yermolay pulled his gun, aiming at Keely.

"I wouldn't do that if I were you," he said.

She rushed toward Eno's feet to untie him as Tremol dove for the general's arm, slamming him into the wall. The gun went off, hitting the bed a few feet from Eno.

"Shit!" Heart pounding, Keely rushed to untie Eno's feet. Her hands shook, making the task harder. Tremol and the general fought. Tremol got a few hits in before Keely untied Eno's hands.

"Are you okay?" she asked. Eno nodded and they moved to the door, while Tremol and the general threw some punches. Keely found the weapon and got into the general's face, aiming the gun at his temple.

"Stop right there." "You are the only one to blame if Earth is destroyed. Have you no family or anyone you care about?"

Yermolay tensed his jaw.

"I do. I want to live a long, full life. I'd love to get married and have a family and grow old with my husband. And you aren't going to stop me."

Tremol reached for the rope that had bound Eno and tied the general's hands. He grabbed the general and hauled him to his feet.

"You're coming with us, whether you like it or not," Tremol ordered. He pushed him toward the door.

Eno pulled the door opened and a small gray figure stood outside.

"You will release the general and come with me," the strange voice said in Keely's mind."

"Don't listen to the voice!" Tremol shouted. He pushed her away from the alien.

Keely held her breath and aimed at the gray figure, shooting it through the head. She released her breath. "That's for my parents." She stepped over the body and into the hall.

"Now you've done it," Yermolay said.

"What are you talking about?" Tremol asked. He pulled Yermolay through the doorway.

"That was our top EBE you just killed. If I don't report in with him in the next five minutes, number two will shoot down your battleship."

Tremol touched his communicator. "Admiral Esrith, come in."

"Esrith here. Go ahead."

"We have Eno. He is safe. The grays will attempt to shoot down the Concordance in the next five minutes. Take evasive action."

Eno stepped around the body and out into the hall. The others were gathered in the hall just outside the doorway.

"You're going to show us how to get back to our ships or you'll end up like him," Keely threatened the general, poking his head with the weapon.

"This way," He pointed with his head.

Everyone followed the general. Adam and Genesis watched their backs as they moved down the hall. Keely checked her watch and Tremol pulled the general to a halt.

"We don't have much time," she said. Disappointment weighed down on her.

"How much farther?" Tremol shouted at the general.

"Down this hall and through the ramp," he said.

When Keely arrived at the ramp, she peeked through the doorway.

"There are at least fifteen to twenty people in there. How do you expect us to get to our ships?"

"You didn't ask me that. You just wanted to know how to get here," he said smugly.

She wanted to smack that look off Yermolay's face.

"You will order your people to stand down and let us pass or I will personally end your life," Tremol threatened the general.

Tremol stood a few inches taller than the general and was in much better shape, although his mouth bled and his face showed bruises. The general took a second or two before nodding.

Keely pushed open the door.

"Stand down!" Yermolay shouted.

She held the general's gun at chest level, pointing it at every person she came across. Tremol held a hand on the general's throat, pushing him forward with his other arm.

"Drop your weapons!" Keely ordered.

"Collect the weapons," Tremol urged the group behind him.

The councilors, Adam, Genesis and Eno did as they were told. When they got to the ramp leading to the ships, a couple of gray aliens stepped forward.

"**Release the general and come with us,**" they ordered with their minds.

"Don't listen to the voices!" Tremol shouted. The two aliens looked at each member but didn't speak again.

"Move your gray asses out of the way!" Keely ordered. The two aliens looked at her but stood still.

She shot them both in the head.

"Why did you do that? We've been getting all our tech from them," Yermolay said.

"You've been getting the *wrong* tech from them," Tremol said. "They aren't here to help you but to help themselves."

"You're wrong!" The general shouted, pulling against Tremol's hold.

"Their race is dying. They experiment on humans to create a hybrid race. When they have what works for them, you will be destroyed by the very technology they are giving you," Tremol explained.

"No, they've given us HAARP. We can use it now," the general pleaded.

"If that's what I think it is, it controls weather patterns, creating volcanic eruptions, super storms, land quakes, and most importantly, it can control minds," Tremol explained.

"You're wrong!" Yermolay insisted.

"Why were you letting them control you?" Keely asked.

"If we give them what they want, they give us technology."

"Was it worth it?" Genesis asked. "Was it worth trading your own people's lives for your selfish gain?"

An alarm went off.

"What is that for?" Keely asked one of the soldiers standing by.

"The base is on alert. Someone is arriving."

37

CONCORDANCE

*A*dmiral Esrith barked out his orders. "Shields up! Monitor the frequencies we've found."

"Admiral, a spike in the frequency in the area above the White House," Captain Melbus reported.

Esrith glanced at the vid-screen showing where his people were on the northern continent. In the state of New York, an island to the right of the map showed where the frequency rose to a high measure. "Fire on that spike!" Esrith ordered.

Within seconds, a bright flash appeared and then the island was gone.

"Another spike, sir!" Captain Melbus pointed out.

This time, the spike occurred in one of the tunnels under the Earth. "Fire on that spike, Captain!"

"Yes sir."

Moments later, a shock wave recorded on the vid-screen, showed the collapse of a large network of tunnels across the upper part of the United States.

"Pinpoint the remaining tunnels, Captain. We're going to show the grays they can't have this planet."

Keely led the group down the ramp to the holding area where the ships were. "Load everyone into the ships," she said.

Genesis and Adam, along with the two councilors, got into Shadow One.

Soldiers surrounded the two ships as Keely was the last to enter Shadow Two. The general was inside with Tremol and Eno.

Eno took the pilot's seat while Tremol secured the general to a back seat. Keely sat beside Eno. "Anything I can do for you?" she asked Eno.

"We're all set, just holding for Genesis in Shadow One. She's first in line to leave."

But Genesis didn't leave. Something was blocking her.

"Tremol to Admiral Esrith, come in."

"Esrith here."

"We're about to leave the underwater base."

"You're good to go, Tremol. We have eliminated the grays' threat and we are destroying all their tunnels."

"No!" General Yermolay shouted. "That's not possible."

"I told you it was possible if you were dealing with the grays," Tremol said.

A comm-link opened up and another voice came through.

"This is Space Force Command to Shadow Two, come in."

"Shadow Two, go ahead," Eno said.

"We are below you at the underwater base. We will escort you back to the White House."

Eno looked at Tremol. "What is your plan, sir?"

"We follow the Space Force. We'll need to communicate with their leader before heading back to the Concordance."

"Yes sir. Eno to Space Force Command, ready to go. Lead on."

Within minutes, Shadow One took off and Eno followed.

"You have a lot to answer for, General," Keely turned to address him.

"I answer to no one."

"We'll see about that." Keely picked up her phone and noticed a missed call. She dialed the familiar number.

"Hi, Mom. Is everything all right?"

"No, honey. I was worried about you. It's all over the news."

"What is?"

"How aliens landed at the White House and you were escorting two aliens in search of a landing party."

"What?"

"It was first seen in a Washington newspaper, written by David Staples."

"My David?"

"Yes, now it's all over the TV stations."

"Oh my gosh! How could this happen?"

"That's not the worst of it, honey. Your father and I both have implants in us. Your father's is in his leg and they set up a surgery date for him."

"What about you?"

"My implant is in my brain. They say it's inoperable from where it's located."

"No!"

"Yes, I'm afraid so. The President's about to speak, honey. I'll call you back."

Keely's heart dropped. How could this happen? She ran her hands through her hair, panic setting in.

"What's wrong?" Tremol asked her.

Keely pulled up a news feed on her phone and listened

in horror as her world came crashing down on her. She held up the phone so everyone could hear.

"First of all, we have aliens visiting this planet as we speak. They came in peace to share technology and open trade between their system and ours. That's a good thing. But what happened is a secret arm of our government took it upon themselves to abduct these visitors and hold them hostage. Our Space Force, which I thought I was forming, has been around for about fifty years. Fifty years! Right now, we have sent our best agents in search of these people to bring them to safety. As soon as we have more information, we will let you know. And I assure you, there will be a complete investigation on this incident."

Keely shut off the chatter of voices asking questions.

Her phone rang before Keely could explain anything.

"Hello, General," she said.

"Have you heard the news?"

"Yes sir."

"What do you have to say for yourself?"

"What do you mean?"

"The article said you leaked this information to the press."

"I did no such thing, General."

"How did this information get out?"

"I don't know, sir, honestly."

Tremol grabbed Keely's hand with the ring on it. The hand that held the phone.

"I'll call you right back, sir." She hung up.

Tremol motioned for her to be quiet and slid the ring off her finger. He opened the poison ring and scratched at the surface of the bottom and loosened something. Turning the ring over, he shook out the false bottom.

"What?"

Tremol showed her his hand and the false bottom to the

ring. Underneath it was a bug. Keely pulled out her tool for unlocking doors and dug out the offending piece of technology. Tremol placed it on the floor of the ship and stomped it flat.

"I can't believe it," she said. "David betrayed me."

She turned the phone over and sent a text message to the general.

"I was surveilled by my ex-boyfriend who wrote the article for the Washington newspaper. Here's his address." She finished texting David's whereabouts. Then she copied the information and sent it to her supervisor with additional information. *"Pick him up now. Tell him Keely sent you."*

38

WHITE HOUSE

WASHINGTON, D.C.

The Space Force arrived at the White House in a Zeta Reticulum ship. Shadow One and Two set down beside them. A large contingent of military men and another group of men and women dressed like Keely, surrounded the ships.

By the time the two Vaedran ships lowered their ramps, the Space Force crew greeted them. They were all escorted inside the White House to the Situation Room.

Keely stood with the Secretary of Defense and her supervisor, filling them in on what had happened. Tremol turned General Yermolay over to his people and they handcuffed him. Genesis, Adam, the two Councilors and Tremol stood to one side of the room until the President came to the desk.

"Everyone please be seated," he said.

Genesis flipped on the scanner so that Admiral Esrith could speak as well as hear what was going on in the meeting. She held it on her shoulder, so he could see what she saw.

"As you know, we have been bombarded with allegations from the press about what's been happening. I want to update everyone first, so you know what we've discovered. Afterward, I'll deal with the press."

The Secretary of Defense spoke first.

"I have discovered the Black Government has been behind the abduction of our extraterrestrial visitors as well as trying to destroy the Concordance. They operate under the auspices of the CIA. We have one general in custody now and we expect to question others in this incident by the end of the day. I suggest a full investigation on the CIA, the Black Government, and the cover-up of this information as soon as possible, Mr. President. And I will give you my thoughts on this in writing."

The Secretary of Homeland Security spoke next.

"We will be questioning several people in connection to the conspiracy to keep the technology used against our visitors as well as keeping the technology from other branches of the government. We will also be looking into the destruction of at least seventy-two underground bases that have occurred in the past two hours."

"Seventy-two underground bases?" the President asked.

"Yes, sir."

"What are we doing with all those underground bases?"

"They were all classified as top secret, sir."

"I will declassify all those bases by morning, so you can finish your investigations. Thank you both for your input. I also expect a full investigation of this entire debacle. We will expose the Black Government to the public and dismantle the program. The Space Force will stay intact but will answer to the Secretary of Defense from here on out. All our military branches need to be on the same page."

The Space Force Commander stepped forward. "Mr. President, on behalf of the Space Force, I want to extend our apologies for firing upon the Concordance. We were surprised by their close proximity and fired to deter them from coming closer. In all honesty, sir, we have to admit we have a base on Mars and we are well aware of the Moon Base, which belongs to the grays. We learned later the Concordance had just come out of hyperspace."

"Apology accepted," Admiral Esrith said in a holo-vid.

"This is Admiral Esrith, Mr. President." Tremol stepped forward, doing the introductions.

"Speaking of the Admiral," the President began, "We want to open trade with the Vaedrans." He looked at the Secretary of Commerce. "Set up a meeting for tomorrow," he said.

"Yes, sir."

"We have a situation, sir," another Secretary said.

"What is that?"

"We've had a report of massive earthquakes covering most of the upper U.S. and one in Montauk, New York, and another in Area 51."

"I can explain those," Admiral Esrith said.

"Go ahead, Admiral," the President said.

"We located all the tunnels that were created by the grays along with their high frequency auroral bases. When they shot at us from the first base, we destroyed it, then destroyed the second one before it could fire. Your military is using their electromagnetic technology to manipulate and create weather."

"What do you mean?"

"They can use the weather as a weapon. This technology can do many things, including destroying all electronics but the grays use electromagnetic pulses to control minds."

"Our military was using this technology?" the President asked.

"I can answer that, Mr. President, with a yes. How long they have been doing this is another question," the Secretary of Defense said.

"We can share technology with you that will combat the grays. The grays have a secret agenda, Mr. President, and they won't stop until they've completed it," Admiral Esrith said.

"Oh? And what is that?" the President asked.

"The Zeta Reticulin race, which we refer to as the grays, has been dying. They abduct people and experiment on them to create hybrids. Once they perfect this, they won't need your race anymore and they will use mind control on your people and destroy you with the technology they are sharing with you."

"How do you know this?" the President asked.

"The Pleiadians showed us how to fight the grays since they have tried to take over other planets in the past with no success. We managed to keep them out of our system for decades," Admiral Esrith explained.

"It is imperative that we hold that meeting as soon as possible, to share this information with you," Tremol added.

"Yes, you will be our guests aboard the Concordance for such a meeting, where we can show you some of the technology we are talking about," Admiral Esrith added.

"How many will be attending this meeting, Mr. President?" Tremol asked.

"About twenty-five, I think will be plenty."

"We will send a ship to accommodate everyone at 1000 hours Earth time," Esrith said. "Provided you let our people return now."

The President looked at his Cabinet. "Any objections to this?" he asked his people.

No one responded.

"You're on, Admiral. You can land on the back lawn of the White House," he responded. Then he turned to his Cabinet. "I expect all of you here tomorrow at 9:00 am. Have your questions ready by then." He dismissed them.

As everyone filed out of the door, Tremol gathered his people. "We will leave as we arrived in the respective ships. Everyone ready?"

When everyone nodded, Tremol ushered them out the door. He caught a glimpse of Keely with her head down, standing with her supervisor.

He stopped to thank her for her help and the supervisor left. "McGuire? Are you all right?"

She looked up at him, tears filling her eyes. She shook her head.

"What's wrong?" He turned her to face him.

She took a deep breath. "Because I was careless and let my guard down, I allowed my boyfriend to plant a bug in my ring."

"That wasn't your fault. He betrayed you."

"They are considering disciplinary action against me," she managed to say before the tears streamed down her face.

Tremol reached out and caught her tears on his finger. "I will speak to your supervisor. This is unacceptable. Your government betrayed its people and they will discipline *you* for having a friend who betrayed you? I find this hard to comprehend."

Keely reached up and patted his arm. "Thanks. That's not the worst of it. My mother called earlier and told me she and my father had alien implants. My mother's is inoperable."

"Implants from the grays?"

"Yes, I think so."

"Our medical people can help you. They have experience with this."

Keely blinked a few times and wiped her eyes. "Really?"

"Yes. We are about to leave now. Would you like to join us tomorrow with your parents?"

"Yes!"

"Meet us here at 1000 hours."

She hugged him and Tremol awkwardly hugged her back.

Keely walked outside with Tremol as he joined his group.

His heart lightened to see her perk up.

39

VIRGINIA
COUNTRYSIDE

*K*eely drove straight to her parents' home. It was late afternoon when she arrived.

"Pack your bags, you're coming with me," she said when her mother answered the door.

"What are you talking about?" she asked.

"I'm taking you and Dad to the Concordance where they can remove your implants."

"Concordance?" her father asked. He walked into the room. "Where have I heard that name?"

"Probably on the news."

"Why are you in such a hurry?" her mother asked.

"Because they will send a ship to pick us up at 10:00 am tomorrow morning at the White House.

"A ship?" Her father glanced at her mother.

"These aliens are human. They are here to share technology. They have been fighting the grays for decades and have kept them off their planets."

Her parents looked at her, then each other.

"Come on, let's move it. You're coming with me. You'll stay at my apartment tonight and we'll drive to the White House in the morning."

Both her parents headed for the bedroom and began packing.

40

CONCORDANCE

"*A*dmiral, this is an opportunity to show them how we deal with alien technology," Tremol explained.

"I think you're right. Captain Melbus, get the Chief Medical Officer up here to the bridge."

"Aye, sir."

Moments later, the CMO reported to the admiral.

"What can I do for you, Admiral?" A petite, good-looking woman with almond-shaped eyes and black hair, from Vestra Minor asked.

"Conn, we have some Earthens who will join us tomorrow for a procedure to remove implants placed inside them by the grays. Can your team handle this?"

"We will be delighted, Admiral. We can show our latest surgical equipment to our guests at the same time. Will they be viewing the procedure?"

The Admiral looked at Tremol.

"I'm sure they will have medical people coming to this meeting, Admiral," Tremol said. He hoped that was true. With all the people on the President's Cabinet, surely one of them had a medical background.

"One question, Conn," Tremol began.

She turned and gave Tremol her full attention.

"Will the procedure take a long time?"

"Depending on the location of the implant, the procedure shouldn't take more than thirty minutes. With the prep time, an hour at most." She raised her hand to add a point. "However, the recovery time may take longer, depending, again, on the location of the implants."

Tremol nodded. Keely didn't say where the implants were, but if one was inoperable, it could be dangerous. "Have you ever had one that was inoperable?"

"No. And to ease your mind, I have performed these procedures on other races on different planetary systems where the grays caused the same havoc."

"Thank you," Tremol said.

Conn bowed deeply and left.

"I told you, Tremol, when I thought about what we could be dealing with, I found the best medical people for this trip. Conn has been on numerous trips with the Pleiadians, learning all she could about these gray bastards. Everything will be fine."

Tremol headed to his quarters. He couldn't stop thinking about the Huanti woman he met over twenty-four hours ago. He had only heard about them but had never seen a Huanti up close. There was something mesmerizing about her.

41

WASHINGTON, D.C

*K*eely flipped on the TV once she arrived back at her apartment. Her parents settled into her room and she took the sofa.

"This just in," the reporter began. "There have been several arrests linked to the investigation on the Black Government. The White House reports there will be more forthcoming as the investigation continues. Also, we just learned the reporter who broke the story about the alien secrets has been arrested for illegally wiretapping the Secret Service agent who allegedly leaked the information to him. More on this as it becomes available."

"In other news today, the earthquakes that were felt along the northern part of the United States were the result of electromagnetic pulses aimed at underground U.S. bases. These pulses were fired upon the bases to clear out the auroral frequencies the grays planted there. More on this as it becomes available. And now for the weather..."

Keely flipped off the TV. Nothing about her disciplinary action. She wouldn't tell her parents. They had enough to worry about now with their recent experience with the grays. Those were some creepy aliens. Their faces crept into her thoughts. The voices in her head had been strong, almost paralyzing. If Tremol hadn't shouted to break the link, she may have done what they said.

She thought about Tremol now. He was the most handsome man she had ever seen. His arms were firm, but his touch was so tender when he wiped her tears. It was hard to believe the man was single.

She curled up on her sofa and set her phone alarm to wake early. She would do anything to help her parents.

Although the day turned out differently then she had anticipated, she avoided a galactic war of the worlds. And the Black Government had been outed. Now, it was up to Congress to deal with the criminals who masterminded the plots to keep secrets from the American people. The worst of it was the government was okay with the gray aliens abducting people and subjecting them to experiments. They even made a deal on it! Who gave those men the authority to do such a thing to their own people?

Not only did she feel betrayed by David, but by her own government. And the Secret Service was going to admonish her for the deeds of a creep like David? Her stomach twisted in knots. She ran a hand through her hair and remembered the soft touch Tremol gave her when he ran his hand through her tresses. David had never done that.

Tomorrow seemed so far away. She closed her eyes and thought of the dark-haired man with brown eyes. The feel of his taut body next to hers when they were locked in the storage compartment. She wondered how he would taste.

42

WHITE HOUSE,
WASHINGTON, D.C.

The back lawn of the White House had been cleared of any debris or obstacles. The President paced in his Oval Office, waiting for word from the Vaedrans. His chosen Cabinet members were filing into the room after a short break.

A Secret Service agent stuck his head into the room. "The aliens have landed."

"That's our signal," he said.

The Cabinet members filed out of the room behind the President.

Keely stood at the entrance with her parents.

"I'm sorry, Ms. McGuire, but you no longer have clearance to enter the White House," the agent said.

"What? Why wasn't I told this?"

"Don't know, ma'am."

"I was invited by the Vaedrans."

"I'm sorry, ma'am, but you'll have to leave."

"They are expecting me!"

"I've got my orders."

"By who?"

"Your supervisor and mine."

Her heart fell. How could she contact Tremol? She turned to face her parents.

"I'm so sorry. I didn't tell you yesterday, but they were considering what type of disciplinary action to take against me because of the leaking. I didn't know it would start today."

"Oh, honey. You tried. At least your father still has his appointment for surgery," her mother said.

Her father gave her a hug. "We still have faith in you, Keely. We know this wasn't your fault."

"I've got to figure a way into the White House or at least to the back lawn."

The three of them left the front entrance, walking to the sidewalk. Keely pulled out her phone and called her supervisor, but the call didn't go through. "Damn!"

43

CARGO ONE

Tremol stood at the entrance of the cargo ship, taking names and titles, while Genesis escorted the people to their seats. When the last one arrived, Tremol walked down the ramp, searching for Keely. He used his communicator.

"Hold the take-off. We're missing three guests."

"Got it," the pilot said.

Tremol walked into the White House.

"Hold it right there," a big burly man said.

"I'm looking for Keely McGuire," Tremol said.

"She no longer works here," the man responded.

"I demand to speak to her supervisor," Tremol said.

"You demand? And who the hell are you?"

"I am Lieutenant Tremol with the Interplanetary Space Patrol and I spoke to her supervisor yesterday. I need to speak to him at once. The matter is urgent."

The man spoke into his wrist and was wearing earbuds. "He will be here momentarily."

Tom Gowan approached the two of them.

"Can I help you, Lieutenant?"

"Yes, I was to meet Keely McGuire and her parents this morning. Her parents will be undergoing a procedure on our ship, the Concordance. She hasn't arrived. Can you help me contact her?"

Gowan looked him over. "I guess you don't have cell phones, do you?"

"I don't know what that is. I do have a communicator, but Keely does not have one of ours."

The supervisor pulled out his phone and called Keely and gave her instructions. "Come with me," he said.

Tremol followed as the two men headed toward the front of the White House.

"I'm sorry for the confusion. After all the incidents that happened yesterday, Keely has been put on administrative leave."

"What happened was not her fault. She performed her duties in the most professional manner. You will be sorry if you let go of someone with her talents," Tremol said.

"I'm sure we can find someone to replace her. She lacks the confidence she needs to be a great agent."

"I disagree with you on that point."

Gowan stopped and faced a crowd of people. He waved and Tremol saw Keely. His heart lightened. She rushed toward them.

"Thank you for contacting me, sir." She said to Tom Gowan. He nodded.

"Come this way," he said. He led the small group toward the ship.

Once they were away from Keely's supervisor, Tremol grabbed her hand and gave her a squeeze. "I'm glad we found you."

She smiled up at him and he ushered them up the ramp. Genesis led Keely's parents to their seats and Tremol showed Keely to her seat, then sat beside her.

"How did your supervisor get to be in charge?" he asked her. He gazed into her eyes.

"What do you mean?"

"The man is an idiot. He thinks he can replace you."

"He said that?" she gasped.

He nodded and saw her eyes fill with tears.

"I tried, I really tried." She shook her head.

Tremol put his arm around her. "It'll be all right." He kissed the top of her head. He smelled that flowery scent from the day before and wondered if she smelled this good all over. He had to change the subject, or he would be thinking all the things he thought of the night before, which had made it impossible to sleep at all.

"The Chief Medical Officer will perform the procedure to remove the implants. If your parents will agree, then any medical people with your Cabinet members can view the procedure."

"Are you sure he can remove them?"

"He is a she and her name is Conn. She has performed many of these removals on several different races. She assured me she could do it."

She glanced up at him, studying the bruises on his face.

"I didn't thank you for saving my life," she said. She lightly touched his bruises and ran her thumb across his swollen lip. He closed his eyes at her touch, savoring the feelings that ran through him.

"Does it hurt much?"

"A little."

"When I was younger and got injured, my Mom or Dad would kiss my booboos and say a prayer for a healing."

He glanced down at her. "I think I would like that."

She took his face in her hands and gently kissed his bruised cheek. "I pray for a healing for you in the name of

Jesus." Then she lightly kissed the side of his swollen mouth. "I pray for a healing for you in the name of Jesus."

"Thank you," he said. He lifted her chin up and kissed her back.

44

CONCORDANCE

*A*fter arriving on the Concordance, the President and his Cabinet were ushered into a large meeting room with Admiral Esrith, the councilors, and all the scientists and military people.

Tremol ushered Keely and her parents into the med-bay where the CMO waited with her staff.

"Keely, this is Conn. She will be taking care of your parents. Conn, this is Mr. and Mrs. McGuire," he said.

Conn bowed and introduced her staff, then herself. "I am a healer and the Chief Medical Officer. We will need scans of both of you to determine how to proceed."

"Sure," Mr. and Mrs. McGuire said.

"Come this way," Conn gestured. "You two can wait here."

"Will we have time for a tour of the ship?" he asked.

"Yes. I will call you when we are ready." She gestured to her communicator.

"Come on, Keely, I'll show you around," he said. He grabbed her hand and held on as they walked around the different decks. Her hands were small, but strong for a woman. He liked her spirit. She seemed to perk up since she first learned that she was replaceable. The thought made him angry at her supervisor.

When he finished showing her the ship, they headed back to the med-bay.

"What will you do if you don't go back to the Secret Service?" he asked.

"I'm not sure. I once had a summer job where I worked in a resort, helping guests. I really enjoyed it. It's totally different than law enforcement, but now, I don't know. I feel numb all over, like my heart was ripped out and I haven't felt the effects yet."

He gave her hand a squeeze.

"I just hope my parents are okay."

Conn walked into the waiting area. "We have located the implants."

"Can you tell if they are from the grays?" Keely asked.

"I know of no other group of aliens who work this way. It is understood by most species, that when arriving on a foreign planet, you do not mess with the local inhabitants. It seems the grays are the only ones who don't understand this law."

"Does it look like you'll be able to remove them?" He asked.

"Yes. We have performed both types of procedures in the past with success."

Keely hugged Conn. "Thank you."

"It is not over yet," Conn said. "If you have others who wish to view this procedure, please let them know we are ready to proceed."

"Will do," he said. "I'll be right back."

He headed straight to the meeting room and was announced to the group. "Conn is ready to proceed with the removal of alien implants. Do any of you wish to view this procedure?"

Three people raised their hands. "Come with me."

The four of them arrived at the med-bay where they suited up and went to the viewing area above the table. He stood beside Keely and held her hand while they watched.

The first one on the table was Mr. McGuire and he was unconscious. His procedure took a couple minutes to cut open the leg and pull the piece of alien metal out. Conn then prayed over the open wound until it sealed itself shut and completely healed over with no scarring.

"What did she just do?" Keely asked.

"She is a healer. She prayed in her native tongue for a healing and it was done."

"I don't understand?"

"It is a matter of faith. Healers cannot remove things, but once removed, they can heal the tissues around the cut or injury with prayer. Genesis is a healer as well."

"Oh."

"He will sleep for a while and when he wakes, he will be fine," Conn said.

Medical staff wheeled the bed Mr. McGuire was on into a room with another staff member to monitor him.

Another staff member wheeled Mrs. McGuire into the room.

"To remove this alien piece of metal from the brain area, we will go in through the nose, just like the grays did to place it there," Conn said. She used a sophisticated tubing while using a scanning device to show her where the tubing was going. She inserted it into Mrs. McGuire's nostril and forced it up until it was beside the object. Then, using a handle at the end of the tubing that was attached to the scanning device, a small pincher-like device came out through the tubing and grabbed the object and then retracted the same way it went in.

He glanced over at Keely and she held her nose while

watching. Once the object was clear, Conn prayed over Mrs. McGuire in the same manner.

"She will sleep longer than the first person since the object was implanted so far into her cranium area. This is normal."

A staff member wheeled Mrs. McGuire into the same room as Mr. McGuire.

"Both people will be monitored while they are here and can return home tomorrow. We are now finished. If you have any questions, I will be available to answer. Thank you." She bowed.

"That's it?" Keely asked.

"Yes. It's that simple. Those two items they removed are used by the grays to locate and track the people they are implanted into. That's why they revisit the same people multiple times." He led Keely out of the viewing area and met up with Conn in the cleansing area of the med-bay.

"The grays can speak to their victims telepathically, through the implants, making them obedient, like mind control," Conn said.

The three other people who had viewed the procedure joined them to speak to Conn personally.

Keely hugged him tightly. "Thank you," she said.

"You will stay aboard the Concordance while your parents are here," he said.

"Is there room?"

"Yes, we can accommodate up to fifteen more people if we have anyone returning with us to Vaedra."

"I guess the President will make that call when the time comes," she said.

His communicator went off and he answered. "Tremol here."

"Meet me on the bridge in five minutes," Admiral Esrith said.

He and Keely removed their protective suits and headed for the bridge.

"Yes, Admiral?"

"Looks like we've got some negotiations going on. We'll be staying here the remainder of the week while the scientists and medical people show the Earthens their techniques and equipment."

"That's what we wanted, isn't it?"

"Yes. I'll be going over some things with the Secretary of Defense and his top people. We may have some guests accompanying us back to Vaedra to purchase some ships. The Space Force is interested in what we have."

"Is there anything you need or want me to do, Admiral?" he asked.

"I've got most of the pilots on training missions with the Space Force and some Air Force pilots the next couple of days, so I'll need you to shuttle our guests back and forth in the Cargo One. I have Genesis and Adam on the Cargo Two if needed."

"Yes, sir. Just let me know when you want me, and I'll be there."

"Our guests will be ready to return to Earth in about an hour. You'll stay there and return in the morning by 0900 hours."

"Uh, yes sir. You want me to stay aboard the Cargo One?"

"There's room in the cargo hold for sleeping. I'm sure you've done that a time or two."

"Not in a long while, sir."

"You can stay with me," Keely said.

Both men turned toward her. She had been so quiet, he had forgotten she was there.

"I don't want to impose." He was taken aback by her offer. But he would give anything to spend more time with her.

"Don't be silly. My parents stayed there with me last night and they're going to be here tonight. I'll come back with you in the morning."

"I don't see a problem with that? Do you, Tremol?"

"Uh, no sir."

"All right, then. Be at the docking bay in an hour."

"Yes, sir."

45

CARGO ONE

*T*remol and Keely waited at the entrance of Cargo One while the dignitaries filed onto the Cargo ship.

When the President was about to step on, Keely stepped forward to talk to him.

"Mr. President, I want to apologize to you for what happened with the leaking. I didn't know I was bugged, and it came from me. I am truly sorry. I would never have done a thing like that on purpose. I value my job as a Secret Service agent," she said.

"I appreciate your apology, McGuire. It's really hard being in a position of trust and finding out you were betrayed by someone you trusted. I feel I let down the American people because I trusted others in the government before me and they betrayed me and the whole country. I'll make this right. We have to make this right."

"Yes, sir." She stepped back to let him pass.

Once everyone was inside, Tremol turned to her.

"I could use a co-pilot," he said.

"Me? I don't know anything about flying."

"I'll show you." He pulled her along into the Nav-U-Com and closed the ramp using the scanner.

"Stay here, I have to alert the others about their safety harnesses and I'll be right back."

He stood before everyone and explained about using the safety harnesses, then returned to the Nav-U-Com.

"Okay, buckle in," he said.

She did as he instructed. "Now what?"

"This is pre-flight." He showed her each step as he explained it and had her do it with him. Finally, everything checked out and he started the engines.

The hangar bay opened, and they flew out and down toward Earth. It took a matter of minutes before the Washington skyline came into view. He set the ship down on the back lawn of the White House and grabbed the scanner.

"Come with me," he said.

Keely followed Tremol to the door and watched as each person descended the ramp.

"Mr. President, will we be able to get clearance for this week to park here and be able to come back here each day?" Keely asked.

"I'll get you clearance, McGuire, don't worry," the President said.

When everyone was off the ship, Tremol locked up and took the scanner. "Where to?" He tried to contain his excitement. Being alone with Keely was exciting enough without all the other sensory things going on.

"My car is parked down the street," she said. They walked toward the parking lot.

"Now you can see how Earthens live," she said.

"I'm looking forward to it." He winked.

Keely put the top down in her car. "I want you to experience what it feels like to drive in a convertible."

"This is actually quite nice," he said. He got comfortable in her front passenger seat.

She pulled her hair out of its bun and let the wind run through her hair. "I love it, too."

After a thirty-minute ride, they arrived at her apartment.

"This is where I live, Tremol," she said. Keely unlocked her door and ushered him inside.

"I'll change the sheets for you," she said. She opened a door and pulled some colorful cloth out and set it on a chair.

Keely removed the sheets from the bed and placed them in a hamper. Then she made the bed with the new cloths. He helped her.

"This is similar to how we sleep on Vestra Major," he said.

After they finished the bed, Keely picked up her phone and dialed a number. "You need to try pizza while you're here," she said.

She took him by the hand and gave him a tour of her dwelling. "This is the kitchen and dining room." She opened a large box. "This is my refrigerator," she showed him the contents. "Oh, great! We have wine to go with the pizza."

"This is my living room." She waved her hand at the space a few feet away from the kitchen. "I'll be sleeping here," she said, moving the cloths off the couch. She patted the seat.

"Sit," she ordered.

"This is not very comfortable for sleeping," he said.

"It'll do for tonight." She moved to a table with a large vid-screen and several small boxes underneath. She turned a knob and music played.

"Do you dance?"

"Dance?" He wasn't sure what she meant. She pulled

him by the hand and moved his hand in the air and held it with hers. She put his other hand around her waist and started moving to the music. He had seen people on Vestra Major move to music, but their bodies didn't touch. This was new to him and sent strange sensations throughout his body.

"We call this dancing," she said. He tried to follow along.

"I find this pleasant," he said. He felt her arm pull him closer around the waist and his body reacted to her touch. Then her other hand pulled his hand to her chest. Then she reached up on her toes and pulled his face to hers.

He scooped her up in his arms and kissed her. Her arms were around his neck and she kissed him back. He didn't want to stop. He had never gone this far with a woman.

A bell rang, and he stiffened.

"Pizza!" She reluctantly pulled away to answer the door. She gave the man at the door some kashis and he gave her a box.

"We can continue where we left off after pizza," she said.

"The thought has me intrigued," he said.

She laughed. Hard.

"What?"

She shook her head and poured each of them a drink of a pink beverage. She sipped hers. He tried his drink.

"Inebrium. I've had this before."

"It's wine, but I guess it could make you inebriated if you drank enough of it."

He ate the pizza and drank more inebrium. "This is quite nice. I think I like it here."

She laughed.

After the pizza and inebrium were gone, she pulled him up to dance. He tried moving to the music, but he couldn't get his feet to move right. She laughed more. He kissed her, and she stopped laughing. When she came up for air, she pulled him to the sleeping compartment and removed her shirt. She had the tiny brown spots all over her body. He touched her shoulder and found it was soft.

"You kiss like a human," she said.

"That's because I am a human."

"Do you have other parts like a human?" She tugged at his clothes. It dawned on him what she was asking and dropped his unicrin on the floor. Within minutes, he showed her just how human he was.

46

WASHINGTON, D.C

*K*eely woke up in Tremol's arms. She had no regrets but a lot of mixed emotions. She rubbed her hands up and down his firm abs. Yes, he was all human and more than she expected. She didn't want him to leave Earth, but he was here on a mission. His time was limited, and he would soon go back with all his people.

Her alarm went off. "What is that?" he asked.

"Time to get up." She kissed his cheek.

He rolled over on top of her. "I like it here."

"I like you being here," she said. She kissed him again, only this time, he reciprocated until they made love.

"We have to be at the White House to pick up those people at 0900 hours. We need to get moving."

Tremol sat up quickly. "How much time do we have?"

"If we shower quickly, we can make it in plenty of time." She headed to the bathroom and started the shower.

"Come on, we'll have to shower together to get done in time."

He joined her but acted as if it was all new to him. Her shower was not that big, but they managed to finish without hurting each other. With all the kissing, she managed to keep him from making love to her again.

"I think I unleashed something within you last night," she said.

"You did." He gave her a wicked smile and a wink.

She put on a clean suit like she used to wear before going to uniform division and he dressed in the same uniform he wore the day before.

She strapped on her Sig and holster, grabbed her keys and phone and headed for the door. Tremol followed her out.

She pulled her wet hair back into a pony tail and let the top down on her car. "This is how I dry my hair," she said. They were off in the convertible, headed for the White House.

"When we go back to Vaedra, you will come with me," he said.

"What?" She glanced at him while she drove.

"Yes. We are mates now. You will come with me and live on Vestra Major."

Her heart pounded. The thought of leaving her parents and of leaving her job all hit her at once. "I...my parents are here. I have a job here."

"Your parents are welcome to come to Vestra Major. Your supervisor wanted to replace you. You can do better on Vestra Major. The I.S.P. could use someone with your skills."

She glanced at him and then the road. "Mates?"

He leaned over and caressed her face. "I want to spend my life with you."

"But we don't even know each other," she confessed.

"We did, last night."

She swallowed hard. He had a point. And she enjoyed every minute of it. Had she just changed her life forever, with one night of passion?

They arrived at the White House with a few minutes to spare and raced to the entrance.

"The President said he would give me clearance to come and go with the Cargo One," she said to the agent.

He checked both of them for weapons.

"You'll have to surrender your weapon," the agent said.

"What? Why?"

"Part of your disciplinary action. I'm sure it's only temporary."

"I want to speak to Gowan," she said.

"He's not here but those are my orders." He showed her the notes on his clipboard. She handed Tremol her phone and keys, then removed her jacket. She reluctantly removed her weapon and holster, fighting back tears. She worked hard in college to get to the point of being hired by the Secret Service, then worked even harder throughout the training. Giving up her weapon was like giving up a piece of her heart.

Tremol didn't have a weapon, so the agent handed her two badges and ushered them through. "The aliens have landed," the agent spoke into his radio.

Tremol opened the ramp and Keely ushered everyone inside. After they were all aboard, Tremol reminded them to strap in. He and Keely stepped inside the Nav-U-Com. Tremol went over the pre-flight with her and she followed his direction.

"Hmmm, this isn't so bad," she said.

"I think with practice, you could fly a smaller ship. I can teach you, if you want?"

"Sure, when we get to Vestra Major," she said. Was this really happening? Or was it a fantastic dream? Maybe she could get use to this.

He smiled and started the engines. He had a nice smile, she realized.

"I'm sorry for what happened to you this morning," he said.

Thinking about it made her eyes well up, so she nodded instead.

"I trained long and hard for the I.S.P. My friends and some of my family didn't think I would make it. But I was determined and kept studying, working my body to be fit just to go through their training."

"But you made it," she whispered.

"Yes, but I felt your pain when they took away your weapon. I know you trained long and hard as well." He patted her arm. "We are a team now. We will work this out together."

"Thank you." She held onto his arm that held her arm. Her heart lightened at his words. She was no longer alone in this world and it felt good.

Within thirty minutes, they were back at the Concordance.

She supervised everyone off the ramp and then headed to the med-bay to see her parents. Tremol remained behind to speak to the admiral after the admiral greeted the dignitaries.

"How are you both feeling?" she asked. Her parents were finishing a meal in the room they were assigned.

"I feel great," her mother said. "The headaches are gone and no more voices in my head."

"I haven't had any nightmares either," her father said.

She hugged them both. "I have some news for you," she said.

Her parents looked at her expectantly.

"Tremol asked me to go to Vestra Major with him and be his mate."

"His mate?"

"That's what they call it instead of marriage."

"Oh, my! No wedding?" Her mother said.

Tremol walked into the room. He glanced at her parents and at her. "Did I miss something?"

"I told them you wanted me to be your mate and live on Vestra Major," she explained.

He turned to her parents. "You are both welcome to come to Vestra Major to visit or to live. I will work it out."

"Don't you have a ceremony or something for the occasion?" Her mother asked.

"Yes, we do. We can even have the admiral perform the mating ceremony."

"When you put it that way, it sounds obscene," her father said.

Tremol's eyes grew large. "No, it's sacred! We exchange vows and the admiral would tie our hands together as we do that, and we get the blessing of our parents. Only my mother lives now and the two of you."

Her parents looked at each other. "This is all so sudden," her mother said.

"Mom, you didn't like David and you never met him. Tremol got you both healed and the implants removed. At least give him a chance. He did that for me because I love you," she said.

"I did it for you because *I* love *you*," he said to her. He lifted her chin and gave her a kiss.

"I love you, too." And she meant it.

The Admiral stepped into the room. "I cleared my calendar, Tremol. I can perform the ceremony today, on the ship, or next week, when we get back to Vaedra."

"Today would be nice," she found herself saying.

~

Hours later, while the crew and dignitaries enjoyed a dinner break, Tremol, both her parents and Keely were in the admiral's private suite.

"I asked Eno to be a witness," Admiral Esrith said. "He should be here momentarily."

"Oh, I asked Adam and Genesis," Tremol said.

"I'm good with that, Admiral, if that's okay with you?" Keely asked.

"It's perfectly fine."

When the three of them arrived, Genesis placed a small wreath of flowers around Keely's head. Her hair was loose and free, the way Tremol liked it.

"Thank you."

"Tremol and Keely, you understand that this ceremony binds you for life?"

"Yes," Tremol said.

She nodded. "Yes."

The admiral bound their wrists together with a small leather cord and recited a passage from a book he held in his hands. "The leather cord signifies the trials you will face together in your new life," the admiral said. He motioned for Eno to step forward. Eno held a large, lit candle. Genesis handed a candle to her and Adam gave one to Tremol.

"The candle signifies the faith and hope you must have to get through these trials. Light your candles."

Both she and Tremol lit their candles from the flame of the larger one Eno held.

Adam stepped forward and handed Tremol something.

"Place the ring on your mate's finger," the admiral said to him.

Tremol took her hand and placed the ring on her middle

finger. Then Genesis handed something to her. It was a colored ring.

"Now place your ring on your mate's finger," he said to her.

"The middle finger?"

"Yes."

She did as she was told. Her nerves got the best of her and her hand shook a little.

"The colors stand for longevity, health, prosperity, fertility, peace and love," the admiral said. "I declare you as mates before these witnesses. Live long, love well, and prosper."

Tremol blew out his candle, so she did the same. Then, he kissed her. A sweet kiss that promised more to come.

Mrs. McGuire wiped a tear from her eye. "That was so sweet."

"And simple," her father said. "I like that."

"You may remove the cord when you two become one," the Admiral said.

She blushed and Tremol saw it. He lifted her chin.

"Don't you love the color she changes into when she is embarrassed?"

She felt her face grow even hotter. "Stop it!"

Adam patted her on the back. "Welcome to the club."

Genesis put her arm around Adam. "I love to make him change colors, too."

"We have a meal prepared for everyone in here. It should arrive shortly and then it's back to work," Admiral Esrith said.

Tremol managed to slip away with her to his quarters. Once they were alone, he kissed her passionately. He tasted salty, and sweet. His kisses sent a heat running through her and a need she wanted to fill, but their hands were still bound, and his bed was small.

"I think we should wait until we get back to my place," she said.

He glanced at the bed. "I agree."

She raised her hand that was tied to his. "Let's take care of this, first.

He found a knife on his desk and cut them free. She wrapped her hands around his neck. "I don't even know your last name," she said.

"I only have one name, since my father no longer lives."

"Tremol?"

"Yes."

"Will I still be Keely McGuire, then?"

"You will be Keely of Tremol. *My* Keely, now and forever."

47

CONCORDANCE

*W*hen the time came to load up the dignitaries, Keely brought her parents to the Cargo One.

"I think we'll have plenty of time to get home tonight once we pick up our car at your apartment," her father said.

"I'm so glad Tremol arranged for the removal of your implants."

"We are too," her mother said. Keely hugged her mother and father, then led her parents up the ramp to their seats. She returned to her post at the bottom of the ramp.

Most of the dignitaries had boarded except the President and a couple other people. She noticed Admiral Esrith walked with them to the hangar bay.

"Agent McGuire," the President began, "our trade talks are coming along nicely but I think we're going to need someone like you to be a liaison for Earth and for the Vaedran side of things."

Tremol walked up to the small group.

"I would have to check with Mr. Gowan, sir, since he's my supervisor," Keely said.

"What you're doing now seems to be working fine, but I'm talking about when we have groups visiting Earth from the Vaedra System, we'll need someone to oversee aspects of it, like meals and accommodations, transportation and such. And we'll need someone on the Vaedra side to do the same thing for us."

"I would love that, Mr. President. When do I start?"

"I'll talk to Gowan tonight and set it up." He looked at Tremol. "You *are* going to be my Vaedran liaison, aren't you?"

"Yes, sir." He looked at the President and then at the admiral. "I'm not sure who I would report to."

Contor walked up. "I'll take care of that, Tremol. I'll speak to the council. We may be able to operate a jointly funded program for both of you since these trade talks will continue in Vaedra and perhaps back here. We might even persuade the Pleiadians to join us."

"In that case, I think we'll need a bigger ship." The President said.

"Yes, you will, but you can't have mine," the admiral said.

Everyone laughed.

"Everyone is accounted for," Keely said.

Tremol handed her the scanner and she closed the ramp. She then helped him with pre-flight and they were off.

"Your President knows the value of a good worker when he sees one," Tremol said.

"We're doing this together, as a team," she said. She touched his shoulder.

"Yes, my Keely, we are."

ALSO BY ESTER LOPEZ

AFTERMATH, BOOK 4 IN THE VAEDRA CHRONICLES SERIES

*a*tlantic Ocean, Off the Coast of Florida

"I got a big one, Dad!"

"Fight it, Jimmy. Don't lose it. Eddie, get the gaff hook."

Eddie moved behind his brother to grab the gaff. A strange light, moving rapidly underwater toward their boat, caught his attention. What would be out here late at night? Eddie pulled out his phone and started filming it.

Dave moved behind Jimmy to help him hold onto the pole. "Eddie! Where's that gaff hook?"

"Dad! Look at this!" Eddie shouted.

Dave glanced toward Eddie. The ocean lit up around the boat. Dave was thrown off balance as Jimmy fell into his arms. One hand was around his son, the other held the pole. Dave swung his attention to the bow of the boat as it lifted out of the water. He and Jimmy fell back against the cabin. The giant grouper fell on top of Jimmy, thrashing and kicking. Before them, a space ship wider than six cabin cruisers lifted out of the water with two more ships on each side of it.

Their boat slammed back into the water.

"Eddie? Are you all right?"

"I got it, Dad! I got it on my phone."

Before he could show his dad the film, more lights came toward them from under the ocean.

Eddie turned around and filmed it. This time, the space ships did not lift the boat, but came out farther ahead of them in the water. These five ships were about the same size as the first five.

"Call the Coast Guard, Dad," Jimmy said.

"Who is going to believe it, son?"

Eddie took a picture of Jimmy with his fish. "I sent it to the local news. They'll believe the film footage, Dad. This is news!"

Altay Mountains, Russia

A group of hikers on an outing looked up at the mountains and saw six UFOs fly out from the mountain range and head up into space. One of the hikers pulled out his camera and took pictures of the ships before they disappeared.

Virginia Countryside

Mr. and Mrs. McGuire sat in their living room and watched the news reports about the alien exodus.

"I think we should go and stay at Keely's apartment in D.C.," Mrs. McGuire said.

"Why? We've had the implants taken out."

"Yes, but they may still find us. They know where we live."

Mr. McGuire stood up. "You're right, honey. We better start packing."

Situation Room, White House, Washington, DC

"The latest reports from around the world shows a mass exodus of space ships heading into space. Here are some images from Russia. Then we have some from the Pacific Ocean and the Mediterranean Sea. The last is a video from the coast of Florida."

The President and his key officials watched the screen as a newscaster reported. The president sat forward in his seat.

"Has General Yermolay decided to talk?"

"He's talking to his lawyer, sir," his aide replied.

"This secret government stops now. This thing Truman started has snowballed into a giant mess. Now we have these aliens, living on our planet, secretly working with a select few for the benefit of that select few. I want answers and I want them now. If we have to arrest everyone involved to get answers, then so be it. The future of this planet is at stake and it all falls back on this secret government."

"I believe the DOJ have arrested about forty people so far, sir."

"Someone needs to start talking. The aliens are planning something and it doesn't look good."

Space, The Concordance

Captain Gadara ni Hovsep sat at her Nav-U-Comm, watching the six pilots take turns landing their class A wing ships, otherwise known as military escorts, into the Concordance's landing bays.

"Easy and steady. There you go. Good job! Next!"

She could see the four remaining pilots holding behind the Concordance, waiting their turns.

She had already taught them how to fly the wedges and these military escort ships. All that was left were the transporters. When this group finished their tour with the Concordance, she would finally get her promotion to Mission Specialist and be in the next Exploration Group, leaving the Vaedra System. She had done everything she set out to do with the military. Anything higher than Captain in the military meant more paperwork and she refused to do any more of that. Now, she wanted more action.

She wanted to see what else was out there. The Earth system seemed interesting enough, but that planet was well populated. Did they even explore their own system? Were there people on the other planets rotating around their sun?

She didn't get her questions answered because she had been training these six new pilots for the Vaedran Military. While Admiral Esrith had the Concordance hovering over Earth, waiting for his mission to end, she had her own mission.

These pilots seemed ready. They took all the sim training and manual training she gave them. This last part was actual flight training maneuvers, most of it spent flying around Earth and its moon. Every scenario she could think of, she threw at them, and they handled it well. They tried landings on Earth's oceans and on the moon's surface. It was tense for a while when they lost communications on the moon. And being fired at by those lunar people gave her pilots some live escape practice. Were those lunar people the same people who lived on Earth? Why did they shoot at them? They were just practicing landings on rough surfaces. If their communications hadn't been jammed, the lunar people would have known that.

She was anxious to talk to Eno and find out how the Earth pilots did with their brief training. Were they difficult to work with? Were they fast learners? After his rescue, he took some of the best Vaedran pilots to Earth to train their best pilots.

There was one more flight scheduled for her trainees, but that would be after they made the jump. It would be landing at the Timucan Space Station between Vestra Major and Persus. They had already practiced space jumps, so she was looking forward to the landing. Space station landings could be tricky. Once they passed this test, the rest was all about flight time. If they wanted promotions, they needed to fly more.

Now, she looked forward to some time off. And a tall drink. It was her turn to land. She pulled into the hanger as the Concordance closed up the landing ramp. She waited for pressurization before opening her door.

The rest of her crew gathered around her ship, waiting for orders.

"Okay guys, you're off the next two days. Report to our Sim Room at 0900 hours on Monday." "Yes!" A couple shouted from the group.

"And don't be late!" She couldn't get out of there fast enough. She still had to write up the reports on each man and how they performed for this part of their training. But that could wait. Drink first, paperwork later.

Gadara headed to the Officers Lounge on deck 1. She checked her chrono. It was early. She wouldn't have to put up with anyone at this hour. Most officers showed up after the evening meal.

She took the stairs. The people movers were too slow for her. She had energy to burn and this would help. By the time she got to deck 1, she saw Admiral Esrith walk into the lounge ahead of her.

Damn! She wanted to drink alone. Esrith liked to talk. She moved to the bar on the side away from the admiral.

"Hello, Captain!" Lieutenant Eno ni Esrith said. Eno was taller than his 6'5" admiral father, but with his white-blond hair and pale blue eyes, was otherwise the spitting image of his Chromian parent. Both men were pleasant to look at, but could be very intimidating when they wanted to be.

"Lieutenant," she nodded. "I'll have a Detonator," she said to the barkeep. It was the strongest drink she could tolerate.

"Something must be going on to have three officers in here this early," Lieutenant Eno said as he sipped his drink.

"Something indeed," Admiral Esrith said, moving toward them.

"I'll say," the barkeep added. "This is the fifth Detonator I've made in the last ten minutes.

Gadara glanced at the two Esrith men and the barkeep. "Who are the other two for?"

Before he could answer, the door hissed open and two people stepped inside.

"Lieutenant Tremol and Keely." Admiral Esrith raised his glass to them. "I believe you know Lieutenant Tremol, Captain Gadara?"

"Lieutenant Tremol of the Interplanetary Space Patrol?" she asked. Tremol was definitely Caucus with his dark hair and brown eyes, but he had two inches on her six-foot frame. She'd seen him on the ship before arriving in Earth's atmosphere.

"Yes, and this is his mate, Keely ni Tremol, a Secret Service Agent from the Earthen Delegation. They recently met on Earth and I performed the ceremony here on the Concordance."

Keely was definitely new. She would have remembered someone like her with all that dark orange hair, blue eyes, and all those little brown dots across her face.

"She looks like the Huanti from Plexus," Gadara said.

"That's what Tremol told me when we first met," Keely said. "I know this was a short engagement period. We barely know each other, but I feel as if we get along well, we're both in law enforcement, and we have a lifetime to get to know each other." She glanced at Tremol and smiled.

"They are the first liaisons for the new Delegations between Earth and Vaedra," Lieutenant Eno added.

The barkeep slid two Detonators toward Tremol and one toward Gadara.

Tremol reached for the two drinks and handed one to Keely. Gadara picked up her Detonator.

"May we get to our destination unencumbered." The admiral toasted them.

The five officers lifted their glasses and sipped their drinks when the door to the Officers Lounge hissed open.

www.ingramcontent.com/pod-product-compliance
Lightning Source LLC
Chambersburg PA
CBHW020617120726
47905CB00003B/837